Kira's
ANIMAL RESCUE

By Erin Teagan

★ American Girl®

Published by American Girl Publishing

21 22 23 24 25 26 27 QP 10 9 8 7 6 5 4 3 2 1

Illustrations by Millie Liu
Cover image by Millie Liu · Book design by Gretchen Becker

The following individuals and organizations have generously granted permission
to reproduce their photographs: pp. 128–129—Spenser Platt/Staff/Getty Images
News/Getty Images; Samuel Corum/Stringer/Getty Images News/Getty Images;
Pacific Press/Contributor/LightRocket/Getty Images; Portland Press Herald/
Contributor/Portland Press Herald/Getty Images; Justin Sullivan/Staff/Getty Images
News/Getty Images; pp. 134–135—Courtesy of Luke Hess, Farm Sanctuary and Beth
Lily Redwood; p. 136—Courtesy of Patty Schuchman. All rights reserved.

Cataloging-in-Publication Data available from the Library of Congress

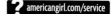
americangirl.com/service

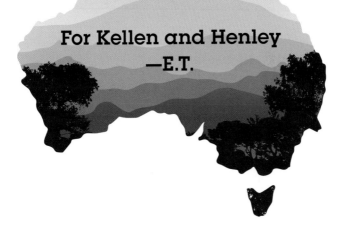

For Kellen and Henley
—E.T.

WITH GRATITUDE TO:

Alison Bee
Doctor of Veterinary Medicine
Queensland, Australia

Tassin Barnard
Walkabout Wildlife Park
New South Wales, Australia

Amelia Lachal and Libby McEniry
Mattel Australia
Victoria, Australia

CONTENTS

1. Fieldmates 1

2. Sirens...9

3. A Do-Something Situation 17

4. A Discovery..27

5. It's a Monster 37

6. The Roundup...46

7. Too Quiet 56

8. Fingers Crossed.......................................62

9. Evacuation 68

10. A Visit to the Solarium...........................76

11. A Perfect Match......................................82

12. The Proof Is in the Picture.....................89

13. Science over Silence 97

14. Facing the Facts 106

15. Dreams for the Future............................116

Global Changemakers...................................127

FIELDMATES

Chapter 1

Alexis and I sat very still on a rock in a far corner of my Aunt Mamie and Auntie Lynette's wildlife sanctuary. Auntie Lynette had told us we could tag along with Evie, one of her graduate students who was studying birds, as long as we didn't get in the way. So Alexis and I were staying as quiet and out of her way as possible on our rock, watching a small flock of Australian red-tailed black cockatoos flutter in the trees above of us.

"Kira," Alexis whispered. "My bum is numb."

"Shhh," I whispered back, trying not to giggle.

Luckily, Evie seemed undisturbed from where she watched the birds, switching between a fancy pair of binoculars and a camera propped on a tripod, taking pictures and taking notes. We were looking for a paradise parrot, a bird we knew would be difficult to find since, technically, it had been extinct for almost one hundred years. But a few weeks ago, Alexis and I were positive we had spotted one in the sanctuary, and we were determined to find it again with Evie's help. So far, even after walking in the bush all day, we'd only managed to find a bunch of wallabies,

a snake that made me jump out of my skin, and about
a hundred parrots that were not of the paradise kind.

I watched the black cockatoos through my own small
pair of binoculars. They were huge birds, bigger than most
of the parrots we saw flying around, and all black except
for a shock of red feathers on the underside of the tail. One
of the cockatoos pulled a large nut off a branch and popped
it open with its sharp beak. *Crack!* The shells dropped to
the ground.

"Cool," I said under my breath.

Alexis groaned. "When can we go back? I'm starving."

Doing science with Evie meant a lot of sitting and waiting, which for some of us—okay, for Alexis—wasn't the
most thrilling activity we could do on the sanctuary. Even
though I had only known Alexis for a month, since my
mom and I first arrived here in Australia to visit my aunts,
we had become close friends. And if I knew anything about
this new friend of mine, it was that she liked action. She'd
rather help her mom in the animal clinic or feed the kangaroos or play with the wombats than watch birds.

For me, the idea that at any moment we could discover
something—a bird or a frog or another kind of animal that
we'd never seen before—was thrilling. Even though my
whole life I had always wanted to be a vet and help wild
animals like my great-aunt Mamie, I was beginning to

wonder whether I wanted to be a scientist like Evie instead.

Out of the sky came a loud bird, chit-chit-chit-chittering at the cockatoos and dive-bombing the big one happily eating nuts. The cockatoos took flight, their squawks echoing throughout the bush.

"That was a male willie wagtail," Evie called to us, stepping away from her camera. "Very territorial species. He must have a nest around here. I've seen those guys even attack dogs when they get too close." She grabbed her water bottle and joined us on our rock.

The little black and white bird sat on the branch above us now, its tail twitching.

"Is it going to attack us?" Alexis asked. "Maybe we should go."

Evie was sipping her water when she froze, seeing something. She brought her binoculars back to her face, and I felt a rush of excitement. Was this it? A big discovery? She walked silently back to her camera, and I held my breath.

"Ughhhh," Alexis moaned. "Bird-watching is so much watching. When are we going to *do* something?"

"This is not boring, for your information," I said, putting my hands on my hips.

She yawned dramatically. "I could really go for a soda water right about now. Or a slice of pavlova. But only if my dad made it."

"How can you think about food when we could be just about to witness a scientific breakthrough?" I asked, but then my stomach rumbled, betraying me. I laughed. "Okay, pavlova cake sounds pretty great right about now."

Alexis's dad was the Bailey Wildlife Sanctuary's head ranger and also probably the best bush cook in all of Queensland. Ever since he got a new hand mixer in the camp kitchen, he'd been whipping up pavlova, a meringue cake topped with whipped cream and fresh berries. An Australian specialty.

"Please tell me you saw that," Evie said, bouncing back over to us, her camera in her hand.

Alexis and I looked at each other.

"The golden-shouldered parrot?" Evie said. "It was right there."

Alexis and I stood up, focusing on where she pointed. "Aren't those birds endangered?" I asked.

"Yes—and they're related to the paradise parrot," Alexis said.

Evie grinned. "You two have done your research. Good on you!"

A few weeks ago, after we saw the mystery bird, Alex and I had pored over her guide to Australian birds to learn everything we could about the paradise parrot. We knew that it liked to nest in termite mounds, that its eggs were round and pinkish white, and that scientists believed a bad drought had caused the paradise parrot to die out. We also read that just in the past few years, there had been several sightings of the bird, although none had been confirmed by scientists. So we were determined to confirm our sighting and prove that the paradise parrot was alive—and living on the Bailey Wildlife Sanctuary.

Evie snapped the cover on her camera lens. "I reckon this will add some nice data to my research paper. Between the black cockatoos and the golden-shouldered parrot, this was a tremendous day out in the field." Evie took a big breath, as if she was taking in all the goodness around her. "Your aunts have really created a paradise out here," she said to me.

"I've been thinking the same thing," I said, smiling.

We admired the gorgeous landscape for a moment, until Alexis said, "Why isn't anyone thinking about cake?"

"All right, all right," Evie said, grabbing her backpack. "Let's go celebrate a good day."

We ate our pavlova with Mr. Curry on the farmhouse veranda, overlooking the bush camp and the rest of the sanctuary. The bush camp was where we ate our meals, on a giant picnic table next to the barbecue and the ring of tents where most of us slept. Alexis and I shared the Wallaroo tent, which was like a bedroom in the middle of the bush: big enough for two beds, a washbasin, a soft rug, and a shelf for our books. We added flowy purple curtains for some extra glam. It was my kind of camping.

"Well, that was delicious, Mr. Curry," Evie said, standing up after finishing her cake.

He gave her a thumbs-up, dabbing his mouth with a napkin. "My pleasure."

"Well, mates, I'm going to sort through the data I collected today," Evie said, stretching. "I'll see you all at dinner." She waved, heading down the path toward her tent at the bush camp. "Thanks for sticking it out with me, Kira and Alex," she called to us over her shoulder. "I couldn't have asked for two better fieldmates."

"Did she just call us her fieldmates?" I asked, nudging Alex with my elbow.

"I think she did," Alex said, popping a strawberry into her mouth.

I grinned. "Evie basically just said we're her partners."

Fieldmates with a research scientist about to discover an extinct bird? Just one more reason to love this place.

SIRENS
Chapter 2

Alex glanced at her watch. "Kira! We've got to go." She took a last quick bite of cake. "We're supposed to feed Blossom." We cleared our plates and then ran, pounding through dry leaves that littered the ground until we reached the sandy path that led to the vet clinic.

Blossom was an orphaned kangaroo joey that we were raising by hand. Alexis's mom, who was the sanctuary's veterinary nurse, kept Blossom in a large pouch-like bag that she wore across her body, just like a mama kangaroo carrying a joey. Now that Aunt Mamie had to take it easy so that she didn't wear out her heart, Alexis and I often took turns taking care of Blossom or feeding her from a bottle, so that Mrs. Curry could do more of the veterinary stuff like shots and stitches and giving medicine.

The top half of the door to the clinic was swung open for fresh air. A giant emu blocked our entrance, its ostrich-like neck poking around and looking for scraps.

"Coming through!" I warned the huge bird. It stepped aside just enough to let us by.

Inside the clinic, Mrs. Curry and two student assistants

sorted through tubs of fresh vegetables piled on a large steel table. Aunt Mamie sat in a rocking chair, feeding a carrot to one of the wombat joeys.

"Did you feed Blossom yet? Can we do it?" Alexis asked, as soon as we stepped inside.

"Good afternoon, girls," Mrs. Curry said, pulling Blossom's pouch over her head and passing the bundle to Alexis. "Did you have a nice day out in the bush?"

Alexis shrugged. "It was okay. We didn't find the paradise parrot yet." She took the pouch from her mom and opened the top. Two pointy little ears popped out.

"Research takes time," Mrs. Curry said.

Aunt Mamie stood up, setting the wombat back into his box in the joey nursery. "Kira, I could use your help in the quarantine room," she said, walking toward the little space off the exam area. It was where the newest arrivals spent their first few hours or days to make sure they weren't carrying any illnesses that could infect the rest of the animals in the clinic.

I followed Aunt Mamie to the corner of the room, where a tiny nylon stocking hung suspended over a heating pad in a small cage. "Pygmy possum joeys," Aunt Mamie said. "Three of them. Tiny itty-bittys."

Through the stocking I could see three little fluffs all lumped together. Aunt Mamie expertly scooped one out

and cradled it
in her hand, the
possum no bigger
than the size of
her thumb. "They
need to stay warm," she whispered. "And fed." She
motioned toward a row of three droppers already filled
with a milky substance. She squeezed the formula from the
first dropper onto a small saucer.

"Look at his little tongue," I said softly, watching the
impossibly tiny animal lick furiously at the milk. "He's so
hungry."

"In a few days when they're a little stronger, you can try
it," Aunt Mamie said.

"Really? You'd let me?" The pygmy possums seemed so
delicate.

"I wouldn't trust most ten-year-olds with this job," Aunt
Mamie said, gently pulling out the next joey, "but you have
a way with animals, Kira."

"I'll be so careful, I promise," I assured her.

Lately, Aunt Mamie had been giving more and more
jobs to me and Alexis. It was because of her heart. She had
been in the hospital a few weeks ago and was supposed
to take it easy around the sanctuary. Originally, Mom and
I had only planned on a two-week visit. But after Aunt

Mamie got sick, we decided to stay the whole summer and help out while she recuperated. Aunt Mamie was supposed to be mostly resting in the farmhouse, but she was terrible at being a patient.

When we finished feeding the tiny possums, I found Alexis outside by the supply shed with Blossom, who was bouncing around in the grass.

"She's out of her pouch!" I exclaimed.

Alexis beamed like a proud mama. "She needs to stretch her legs and get used to being outside now that she's older." Blossom was shaky on her big kangaroo feet, jumping haphazardly, once leaping so high that Alexis grabbed her out of the air before she could fall. "Whoa now," she said with a laugh. "Let's go easy, big girl." Blossom squirmed out of Alexis's grip and hopped toward the hay feeder, pulling out a piece of straw with her teeth.

I sat next to Alexis and took out my binoculars, scanning the field and the walking path that led out to the bush and beyond to the dense trees. The sanctuary was full of wildlife—a paradise for animals—just like Evie said. Kangaroos and wallabies, wombats, echidnas, koalas, possums, and hopefully a paradise parrot.

"Do you think we'll ever find the paradise parrot?" Alexis asked me, as if she could tell what I was thinking.

"Of course we will," I told her. "Evie says it just requires patience." I smiled at her. "Guess that will be easier for some of us."

She threw a handful of grass at me. Blossom bounced over to investigate.

"Well, maybe you and Evie just let me know when you find it. I'll do all the fun stuff like feeding and playing with the animals, while you sit in the bush for hours and hours and hours and—"

"Alex." I was looking through my binoculars again, focusing on a bit of haziness in the sky out in the distance. "Alex," I repeated.

"What is it?" she asked, holding out a piece of straw for Blossom to nibble.

I pulled my binoculars away. "It almost looks like smoke. Way out there."

"What?" She stood up, lifting Blossom back into her pouch and reaching out to take a turn with the binoculars.

I hoped that I was wrong, because one thing I learned from Auntie Lynette was that our property was the driest she'd seen in years. Because of the drought, the fuel load in the bush was high from all the extra leaf litter, fallen branches, and dead trees. In other words, the sanctuary was ripe for a fire.

Alex inhaled sharply. She'd seen the smoke, too. A moment later, we heard sirens coming fast down the road, getting louder and louder, until a fire truck turned into the sanctuary.

We ran toward it, Alexis carrying Blossom in her pouch. By the time we got to the driveway by the farmhouse, almost everyone else was there: my mom, Mr. Curry, Auntie Lynette, Evie, and Aunt Mamie. Mrs. Curry rushed up the path from the clinic, out of breath, pulling off a pair of latex gloves and shoving them in her pocket. "What is it?" she said breathlessly. "Fire?"

Two firefighters were climbing out of a big red and yellow fire truck. "G'day, ma'am," said the fireman nearest to us. He wore heavy pants and a shirt that said "Wallangarra Rural Fire Brigade." He added, "We're just letting you folks know about the bushfire in the area. Started by lightning strike overnight, and despite our best efforts has not yet been contained."

"How big?" Mr. Curry asked. "Where is it?"

"Other side of the river," the fireman said. "It's about a hundred and eighty hectares at the moment." He cleared his throat. "And growing."

Mom, who was standing next to Aunt Mamie and Auntie Lynette, came over and put her hand on my shoulder. "A hundred and eighty hectares?" I asked. "How big is that?"

"About four hundred and fifty acres," Aunt Mamie translated. "Nearly one square mile."

At home it was a mile walk to the smoothie shop from our apartment. It sounded like the fire was about the size of our small town. Fear gripped me.

"Do you have a fire plan?" the other fireman asked.

"We do," Auntie Lynette said, adjusting her wide-brimmed hat against the sun.

"Too many animals on-site not to," Aunt Mamie added.

We did? What was our plan? How much danger were we in? And how would we keep the animals safe?

"Weather appears good over the next few days," the second fireman said. "Calm winds and high humidity will likely keep the fire at bay. But if the forecast changes and the winds pick up, the fire could cross the river before we can control it. That would be the worst-case scenario."

"All we have between us and that river is twenty kilometers of dry bushland," Aunt Mamie said.

"If that were to happen, how long until the fire could reach us?" Mrs. Curry asked.

The fireman rubbed his chin. "If the wind is calm, a day or two. But with strong winds, it could be just a matter of hours, so you'll need to be ready."

I felt a thud in my chest. How did you get ready for a bushfire the size of a small town?

A DO-SOMETHING SITUATION
Chapter 3

After the fire engine drove away, we all stood on the driveway for a few moments, taking in the gravity of the situation. It was our worst fear: a fire when the sanctuary hadn't seen rain in months. It was literally a disaster waiting to happen.

Auntie Lynette clapped her hands. "Reckon we need to get to work. Got ourselves a do-something situation." She sighed, gazing out over the property. From up here, without using my binoculars, the smoke was hardly visible, the sky a bright and cloudless blue. You could almost pretend it wasn't there.

"Mamie," Auntie Lynette said, turning back around, "my dear, how do you feel today?"

"Oh, crikey, Lynette. I'm not at death's door, for Pete's sake," she said, walking over to her. "Just give me a job, will you?"

"All right, then, how about you find temporary carers

for the clinic animals," said Auntie Lynette.

"We're going to send the animals away?" asked Alexis.

"Already?" I said. "But the fire's not that close, right?"

"It's a precaution," Aunt Mamie explained. "Some of our animals will not tolerate the smoke or do well in an emergency evacuation, should one arise. I'd feel better knowing they were already safe off the property." She shot a thumbs-up to Auntie Lynette. "I'll make some phone calls."

"I'll get the transport crates ready," Mrs. Curry said.

"We'll have to start rounding up the wild animals as well," Aunt Mamie said. "We can't have roos and wallabies hopping around still needing to be caught when a fire is approaching."

"I'll start recruiting volunteers in the area to help," Mr. Curry said.

"Do we know how many wild animals there are in the whole sanctuary?" I asked, starting to feel overwhelmed by the task ahead. Evacuating a wilderness vet clinic with animals that had all different needs was hard enough. Adding the wild animals as well seemed impossible.

"We have a roundabout number, bunny," Aunt Mamie said. "We keep track of the regular visitors to the hay feeders, and twice a year we survey the wild ones in the bush with the drone and trail cameras."

Over my shoulder I counted at least five emus walking around. "How big is the whole property?"

"About two hundred acres," Auntie Lynette said.

I felt like I couldn't breathe. There would be hundreds of wild animals in the sanctuary. And every one of them was relying on us for protection.

The next morning, everyone set out right after breakfast to get started on their jobs: Aunt Mamie to find temporary homes for the clinic animals, Mrs. Curry to collect the transport crates, Mr. Curry to find volunteers for extra help. My mom was the weather lady, listening to the radio and watching the online weather station for updates. We all downloaded an app to our phones, set to alert us if the fire crossed the river.

"Make sure you girls pack a duffel with enough clothes for a few days," my mom told Alexis and me. "And whatever else you can't live without. I already packed an emergency kit with Aunt Mamie's medication in case we need to leave quickly."

Emergency kits. Evacuations. My stomach dropped.

Mom reached over and squeezed my hand as she stood up from the table. "Just a precaution. I know how much you like to be prepared."

After she left, I nibbled on my toast for a few minutes and then turned to Alex. "Have you seen Evie?"

Alexis nodded, putting her napkin on her plate and standing up. "Saw her leave for the bush straight from the showers this morning."

"Oh, darn," I said. "I wanted to go with her." I followed Alex over to the compost bin, scraping the last of my breakfast bits. "I don't want to miss anything." I looked beyond the bush camp to the tall trees, where I knew Evie was probably already set up for the day with her camera and tripod and her notebook full of discoveries. "What if she sees the paradise parrot today? Don't you want to be there?"

Alexis blew a strand of hair out of her face. "How about we feed the animals first and then go?"

"Hold up, mates," Auntie Lynette said, getting up from the picnic table. "I need your help around here. Everyone gets a job."

"Like, getting the animals ready for evacuation?" I said. "Alexis and I are really good at animal stuff."

Auntie Lynette scraped her plate and took a final swig of her coffee. "Two strong young sheilas? I can't have you cuddling cute animals right now. I need your muscles." She pounded me on the back. "We need to rake the leaf litter and twigs and other debris away from the buildings and pens. You'll have time to visit Evie later."

Together, we walked toward the shed, navigating around the kangaroos and wallabies lounging under the trees and by the hay feeders. I tried to memorize their features. The one with scruffy fur and black paws. The big one with a darker, reddish coat. I was going to make sure every single wild wallaby and kangaroo, possum and bandicoot, and goanna and snake were evacuated to safety, if the time came.

We stopped by the shed for rakes and then headed toward the animal clinic. "The idea is to create a barrier around the buildings," Auntie Lynette said, demonstrating her raking technique. "If the fire gets close, a spark could land on a dry leaf and spread the destruction."

Alexis and I followed her lead, raking the leaves and dead branches and pine cones away from the pens that surrounded the clinic. It was a huge task. The entire area was deep with debris.

"Did I ever tell you my story of Rosedale?" Auntie Lynette asked, swatting away a fly.

"No," I said.

"What's Rosedale?" asked Alexis.

"When I was your age, my family had a beach house," Auntie Lynette said. "A cozy bungalow in the middle of a gum tree forest. We fed the kookaburras at night. If you bushwalked through the eucalyptus for ten minutes, you came to a cliff overlooking the ocean. From that spot you could see whales breaching and dolphins leaping. A trail led down to the beach, where my friends and I collected shells and played in the surf."

I stopped raking, getting a bad feeling about where her story was going.

"We were unprepared when the bushfire broke out," Auntie Lynette said, no longer smiling. "During a bad storm one day, a lightning strike lit the gum trees, and even though the fireys were there within minutes, it was unstoppable. It was barely noon but the the smoke made it dark as midnight. Everyone escaped to the beaches, and that's where we stayed, choking on smoke, ducking the embers, and watching the town of Rosedale burn."

Alexis and I were silent. Our bushland was so dry, the dirt was cracked. There were no beaches. There was nowhere for us to run. My pulse quickened, and I looked up at the sky. The little cloud of smoke in the distance seemed bigger and more menacing.

"There was this one bloke," Auntie Lynette continued. "He spent days and days fireproofing his house. He raked leaves from his property. Collected twigs and fallen branches. His work was never done. At our own house, we spent our time at the beach and let nature lie. When a tree fell one year in the side yard, we left it. Dad said it would shelter the bugs. Provide a habitat for the spiders, who kept the flies at bay." Auntie Lynette took a breath. Neither of us was raking anymore, only listening. "When we walked back to our houses that day after the fire, our neighbor's was barely damaged. Ours was gone."

"Gone?" I asked.

Auntie Lynette nodded. "Gone. We couldn't salvage anything."

I looked back up the hill at the farmhouse, which had been in my dad's family since the 1800s. It would be devastating to lose it in a bushfire.

"I never knew that you had a beach house, Auntie Lynette. Or that you lost it in a fire." Why hadn't she told me that story before?

She put an arm over my shoulder. "It's not the happiest of stories, dear. But it is one of the reasons that I became a scientist. There is so much to learn about how drought and fire affect our plants and animals. And how it's all tied to our changing climate. I really hope my research and some of the research my students are doing will help protect our land against bushfires someday." She smiled, clapped her hands briskly, and took a big breath. "So, raking. Important. Back to it, girls."

When Auntie Lynette left to check on things back at the farmhouse, Alexis and I took our rakes and a giant rubbish bin to the animal pens near the clinic. Boomer, the wombat joey, scampered out of his hidey-hole, hoping for a carrot. "G'day, Boomer," Alexis said, giving him a scratch through the fence.

"No treats this time," I told him. "We're here on official fireproofing business." The little wombat flipped around and zoomed in the other direction, vaulting over Muffin, another wombat who was sleeping belly-up.

Dexter the parrot, who was already loud on a regular day, was three times as agitated as normal. "Stop your yabbering!" Alexis told him, but the cockatoo kept squawking from inside his cage, standing tall on one of his tree branches. The other parrots looked rather ruffled by Dexter's uproar.

"Dexter!" I called to him. "Shhhhh!"

Aunt Mamie came down the path with her cane. She waved it at the unruly bird. "Everything is okay here, mate!" she said to him. "No need to sound the alarm."

I raked a small pile of leaves away from the parrot enclosure. "Is that what he's doing?"

Aunt Mamie nodded. "Old boy is protecting us. He

must sense danger." She opened Dexter's cage and offered him an arm. "I'll just give him a little break inside."

After Aunt Mamie and Dexter went into the animal clinic, I moved on to rake outside the next pen, the koala enclosure. Mum, the big female koala, munched on eucalyptus leaves from her branch. "G'day, Mum." I felt an ache in my throat, because only a few weeks ago I had spent a lot of time with Mum, trying to get her to bond with Bean, a little koala joey I had helped raise. It wasn't easy, and in the end, Bean had to be transferred to a special koala sanctuary, where there were more koala mamas to teach him how to be a koala. Aunt Mamie had said it was his best chance at survival. I knew she was right, but it was still really hard letting him go.

"He probably misses you, too," Alexis said, standing beside me.

I smiled at her. "How did you know what I was thinking?"

"I always know what you're thinking," she said with a laugh.

I turned away from the koala pen, dragging a branch away from the fence with me. "Oh yeah? Well, I bet I can guess what you're thinking about right now."

"Doubtful," she said, putting her hands on her hips. "I am a complicated and multidimensional—"

"Cake," I said. "You're thinking about cake right now."

She cracked up. "Okay, fine. That was an easy one."

"Yeah, easy for me," I said, because over the past few weeks Alexis and I had become more than just tentmates or two kids who liked animals. We were more like best friends.

Alexis held up her fist for a bump. And then we got back to work, raking until it felt like our arms might fall off.

A DISCOVERY
Chapter 4

B ack at the bush camp, we found Evie on the wooden porch in front of her tent, sorting through her various camera lenses. "Mates!" she said, waving. "I have big news!" A grin took up nearly half her face.

I jogged the rest of the way over. "What is it?"

She finished packing up her camera stuff, zipped her bag closed, and slung it over her shoulder. "I found something that you two need to see right away." She started walking back to the path that led out to the sanctuary, and Alexis and I fell in line behind her.

Evie, this big-time scientist, had something to show *us*? As we followed her, I ran through all the possible scenarios in my head: Maybe she'd found a feather, or some tracks—or maybe she'd even spotted an actual, real live paradise parrot! "Are you going to tell us what it is?" I could barely stand the suspense.

She spun around. "You have to see this for yourself!" And then she launched away from the path into the trees.

"Hey, Kira," Alexis said. "This is where we set up our song meter a few weeks ago."

We came to a little clearing speckled with termite mounds, thick and sturdy towers of dirt as tall as me. "You're right—this is where we recorded the mystery bird-song!" I said. Paradise parrots nested in termite mounds, and this part of the bush was full of them.

Evie turned around, walking backward. "Which is exactly why I picked this area. I looked at your song meter data, and I'm convinced your mystery bird is a paradise parrot. We just have to find it."

About three weeks ago, after Alex and I spotted the bird that we thought was a paradise parrot, we set up a song meter, a little recording box that we mounted onto a stake in the ground. We recorded all the sounds nearby, hoping to catch the song of a paradise parrot. We got the idea from another visiting scientist who was using song meters to capture frog sounds. Later, when we analyzed the recordings, the software identified each of the different birdsongs—except for one, which could not be matched with any of the birds in the giant database. It was a mystery. Or maybe—just maybe—the song came from a bird that was supposed to be extinct, which would explain why it wasn't in the database. At least, that was our hypothesis.

"Okay, walk carefully," Evie said, a finger to her lips as she tiptoed through the maze of termite mounds.

A DISCOVERY

Alexis sneezed. Evie and I both froze as if Alexis had just dropped a dozen eggs. "Sorry!" Alexis squeaked.

"Science is quiet!" I whispered with a snort because we all knew that being quiet was not one of Alexis's strengths.

We continued to one of the far mounds, higher than the rest and dark red. Evie stopped, holding out her arms to keep us back. "Shhhh . . ." She motioned us forward again, the three of us creeping to the other side of the big mound, Alexis holding on to my sleeve. We tiptoed, but even so, our steps were loud with all the dry leaves and brittle twigs crunching under our weight.

When the termite mound was just an arm's length away, Evie stopped and pointed to a perfect hole about the size of a tennis ball. The sight of it gave me goose bumps. A nest!

"Take turns looking inside," Evie whispered. "Just a quick peek."

I bent close to the mound and used my little pocket flashlight, but I could barely see anything. I stepped closer, holding Alexis's hand for balance, and peered directly into the nest. It smelled of earth, like when I pulled weeds out of my mom's garden back home in Michigan. And that's when I saw it. A bright white gleam in the shadows. I gasped. An egg—no, there were three!

After Alexis got a look, Evie pulled us away from the termite mound, and we tiptoed back to the path.

"We don't want to scare the parents away," Evie whispered. "They're probably perched somewhere nearby, watching us."

Back on the path, Alexis started a happy skipping dance, making us all laugh.

Evie asked, "Did you see them? The eggs?"

"Yes—three of them!" I said.

"Plus a feather!" said Alexis. "It was blue—just like a paradise parrot!"

According to Alexis's bird guide, paradise parrots were very colorful, bigger than a parakeet but smaller than a cockatoo. Their wings were black with red shoulders, and their chest and head were this vibrant green and blue color.

"I need to try for a picture," Evie said, biting her lip. "I want to give the nest some space so the parents will come back. I've been watching the nest all day and there's still no sign of them."

Suddenly I felt a wave of worry. There was an out-of-control bushfire just a few miles away. "What if this really is a paradise parrot nest?" I asked. "How can we keep them safe?"

"Right, I thought of that," said Evie. "As soon as I have the proof I need, I'm going to alert a local conservation group that's worked with critically endangered animals before. They'll be able to help us secure the site, monitor their habitat, and evacuate them if needed," she explained.

"What kind of proof?" I asked.

"Are we going to try and catch the bird?" Alexis spun around, clearly hoping for a bird hunt.

Evie smiled. "A picture or video will do just fine."

Alexis let out a big sigh, disappointed.

"It would also be great for the sanctuary," Evie said. "If this is the last known habitat of the paradise parrot, anyone interested in conservation is going to want to support this place."

I glanced at Evie. "You mean people will want to come here to see the bird?" I didn't like the sound of that.

Alexis didn't seem to mind. "I could give guided tours," she said, brightening again.

"No," Evie said. "We'd have to keep its location a secret. Visitors could put the birds at risk. What I mean is a discovery like this would help support the sanctuary by bringing in money and grants."

"And also we'd be famous probably?" Alexis asked, kicking a pine cone out of her path.

"Possibly," Evie said, but then it was clear her thoughts went elsewhere. "Did you girls get an update on the fire this morning? How far away is it now?"

Alex shook her head. "No update yet."

Evie bit her lip. "Just imagine we find a nest of paradise

parrots. The last known existence of an entire species of parrot, and we lose them to a bushfire? I can't let that happen."

"But what can we do?" I asked as a kangaroo hopped across our path and into the trees.

"I think . . ." Evie stopped walking. "I think I need to eat, sleep, and breathe out in the bush. Become one with the wilderness." She looked at us, clapping her hands together. "I'm going to pitch a tent and move out here full-time."

And then she marched on up the trail, Alexis and I jogging to keep up.

"Lynette won't let you move out into the sanctuary with a bushfire just down the road," Alexis said, out of breath.

"She will if she cares about the fate of this bird!" Evie called back.

"Can we sleep out in the sanctuary, too?" Alexis asked, all of us slowing down as the bush camp came into sight.

My stomach dropped. Sleeping in the bush camp on a raised platform, in a comfortable cot, was one thing. Sleeping out in the sanctuary with all the wild animals and creepy-crawlies was another.

"No," said Evie. "I need to minimize human presence. This is important."

Alexis pouted.

"You can visit me, though," Evie said. "My door is open."

"Please don't leave your door open," I told her, because that's how snakes and funnel spiders could get in, and everyone knew they could kill you with one bite.

When we reached the veranda, we followed Evie up the steps and into the farmhouse.

"Whoa," I said. The kitchen had been transformed into a bushfire command center. Auntie Lynette paced in front of a bunch of maps on the wall. Mom was at the computer, scrolling through a website, folders and papers piled around her at the table. In the adjoining room, the television was tuned to the news. A reporter stood in front of a forest, with a bushfire raging in the distance, casting a red glow. Aunt Mamie sat in one of the armchair recliners, an afghan over her legs, a notebook in one hand and a phone in the other.

"Hi there, kids," she said, waving. "Just found a place for Boomer, Daisy, and Muffin." She gave us a thumbs-up, nearly dropping her notebook. "They're getting a helicopter ride to a zoo for a wombat vacation."

"By helicopter?" I repeated. Somehow, picturing the wombats getting airlifted from the sanctuary made the danger and urgency seem more real.

"Professor," Evie said, "I found something very promising out in the bush, and there's reason to believe it may belong to a paradise parrot."

Auntie Lynette stopped pacing and looked at us, surprised. "What did you find?"

"A nest in a termite mound!" I said, unable to help myself.

"With eggs in it!" Alexis chimed in, joining in on my excitement.

Who's bored with bird-watching now, hmm? I thought to myself with a smile.

Evie laughed. "Thank you, mates. And, yes, the girls are correct. I found a nest with three eggs and a blue feather."

"Evie, this is great news," Auntie Lynette said. "Did you see a bird?"

"Not yet," Evie said. "But I wanted to let you know that I'm pitching a tent deeper into the sanctuary to continue my research overnight."

"No," Auntie Lynette said. "It's not safe. Not with a fire so close."

"Professor," Evie pressed, "it's still on the far side of the river. A big river, I might add. Even if the fire were to cross it, we'd have enough time to get out of here."

"It could be only an hour or two if the winds are up, Evie," Aunt Mamie said from her chair. "Fire is unpredictable and unforgiving. It's not smart to be camping out in the bush alone during this time."

Evie held up her cell phone. "I'm just a phone call away. Don't worry, I'll be checking the fire app."

Auntie Lynette shook her head. "Cell phone service out in the middle of the sanctuary is spotty at best."

"But she found a nest, Auntie Lynette!" I said. "What if there's a paradise parrot out there? If you don't let Evie sleep in the bush, and then we never find it again . . ."

"The fire could find it first," Alexis said, finishing my thought.

Auntie Lynette paused, thinking. "Yes, it would be terrible to lose—"

"If there's a paradise parrot here, then it needs to be protected," Evie said. "We can't let them go extinct again."

Auntie Lynette and Aunt Mamie looked at each other.

"How about you set up a research station out there?" Auntie Lynette suggested. "A place to keep your equipment so you can pop in and out easier. If the winds increase or the temperature ticks up, you come back right away."

"Or what if—" Evie started, looking unconvinced.

"Or," Auntie Lynette interrupted, "we can put this research on pause for the time being?"

"Okay, Professor," Evie agreed. "A research station out in the sanctuary, and I sleep at the bush camp."

"And you come back at the first sign of weather, right?"

"You have my word." Evie high-fived Alex and me and then flew out of the farmhouse.

IT'S A MONSTER
Chapter 5

The next morning at breakfast, we smelled smoke, tangy and sharp. We ate our eggs on toast with the distant whine of fire sirens all around us. When the adults went to the farmhouse to finish their coffee and tea with Aunt Mamie on the veranda, Alexis and I hiked into the sanctuary to find Evie's new research station.

"Found it!" Alexis said, pointing to the trees along the path to the termite mounds. Evie had set up a tent for her equipment, and it was easy to spot—bright yellow and glowing like a lantern in the dusty bush. We headed toward it and soon spotted Evie, crouched down and examining some dirt.

"G'day, mates," Evie said. She stood up, brushing herself off. "Tracks. See them?" She pointed at the dirt that she had been inspecting. I leaned over, trying to see what she was talking about.

Evie unfolded a little campstool. "Have a seat." She sat down on a big rock and lifted her binoculars to her eyes. "This is a great time of day for bird-watching. If we sit very still, we might be able to make some good observations."

I pulled out my binoculars from my pocket, staring up into the quiet trees.

Alexis kicked at my shoe. "You always carry a pair of binoculars in your pocket?" she exclaimed, as if that was a remarkable thing to do.

"You don't?" I laughed.

She snorted and then slumped onto the little campstool with a sigh. "How long do you think we'll sit here quietly making observations and not doing anything else?"

Evie turned around. "I reckon we've got a few hours before lunch, right?"

I patted Alex on the knee. "We can share my binoculars."

She popped up out of her chair. "Thank you for that kind offer, mate, but I should probably go check on the animals. Yep. I bet they're needing me right about now." She backpedaled to the trail behind Evie's equipment tent.

I stood up. "Are you sure? Want me to come with you?"

There was a commotion above us in one of the trees, and Evie hopped off her rock, camera in one hand and her notebook in the other. I stood on my toes, trying to see what it was through my binoculars.

"You stay, Kira. I'll see you back at the clinic!" And with a wave, Alexis disappeared down the path.

"Sacred kingfisher," Evie called to me. "Third branch on the right."

I focused my binoculars and found a small blue and white bird, half the size of the parrots I had been seeing all over the bush.

"They also nest in termite mounds," Evie said.

I sucked in a breath. "It has blue feathers, too, so do you think that—"

Evie shook her head before I could finish my thought. "Kingfishers breed much earlier in the season. Our nest is definitely not a kingfisher nest."

I breathed a sigh of relief.

"Good question, though," she said, smiling at me. "You're going to be an excellent scientist when you grow up. You know why?"

Evie thought I was going to be an excellent scientist?

"Number one, you're curious and you ask the right questions," she continued. "Number two, you're a natural observer. And number three, you really care about wildlife."

"Thanks, Evie," I said, feeling my cheeks get warm. "I used to think I wanted to be a vet. Like Aunt Mamie. But lately I've been thinking I'd rather do this kind of science. Research, like you."

Evie grinned. "You'd be great at it."

We stayed like that for a while, both of us watching the bush and waiting for the birds to come back to their nest and take care of their eggs. We observed some kookaburras and a flock of noisy cockatoos, and we even saw a possum scurry across the field station. But after an hour, the birds that belonged to the nest still hadn't returned.

Finally, Evie put down her binoculars and groaned. "I hope I didn't scare them away for good yesterday when I approached their nest." She turned off her camera and closed her notebook. "Or, perhaps the eggs aren't viable. It's July. Most chicks are hatched and flying on their own at this point."

I hadn't thought about that. "You think they might be . . . dead eggs?"

"I really hope not," Evie said. "But sometimes eggs won't hatch when the temperature gets too hot or too cold. And it has been warmer than average these past few months." She thought for a moment and then wrote something in her notebook.

"In that case, do you think the parents would even come back?" I asked.

"I reckon the parents are still around. We'll need to be patient." She looked up from her writing. "And more cautious around the nest. I'm not going to save this bird by being careless."

Later, after leaving Evie at her research station, I found

everyone on the veranda. Mom, Aunt Mamie, and Auntie Lynette were standing over a map rolled out on the table.

"Do you have a fire update?" Mrs. Curry asked, coming up the stairs with Mr. Curry and Alexis. "There's an awful lot of smoke today."

Alex bumped me with her elbow and whispered, "Did you see any paradise parrots?"

"Not yet," I said.

I noticed a series of uneven circles on the map drawn in different colors: a small green one, a bigger yellow one, and an orange circle that was the biggest of all. "What are these?" I asked, pointing to them.

"The progression of the fire, sweetheart," Mom said.

"Crikey," Alexis said, because the fire had gone from 180 hectares to 250 hectares to 400 hectares now, according to the oval-shaped orange blob on the map. The fire had more than doubled in size.

Auntie Lynette pointed to the map. "It made it to the river overnight—which makes this fire only about twenty kilometers away."

That was twelve miles.

"But the forecast is in our favor for now," Mom pointed out. "Low winds, moderate humidity. There's still a decent chance this fire will stay on the other side of the river long enough for the fire brigade to contain it."

I took a breath, not even realizing I had been holding it, and coughed in the soupy air.

Mr. Curry joined us at the table. "Good news. We've got more than twenty volunteers ready to step in and help wrangle up the wild ones should we need it."

"Great, thank you," said Auntie Lynette. "Who else has good news for me?"

Alexis raised her hand. "Kira and I collected at least sixty sacks for the wallabies and kangaroos yesterday."

"Sixty-eight," I said. "We found a jackpot of burlap sacks in the loft of the shed." We'd need them if we ever had to evacuate the wild wallabies and kangaroos, who would stay calmer being transported in a pouch, just like when they were little joeys.

"Mamie has collected those for years," Auntie Lynette said. "Every time we emptied a bag of grain or seed, she'd sock them away."

"And we took all of the extra pillowcases out of the farmhouse," I added.

Auntie Lynette gave us a thumbs-up and turned to Mrs. Curry for her report.

"We've found a place for most of the animals at the Gir-raween Animal Reserve—"

"Even Dexter?" Alexis interrupted. "Do they know Dexter?"

Aunt Mamie smiled. "It's a nice big sanctuary next to Girraween National Park. He can squawk all he wants."

Mrs. Curry checked her watch. "And Boomer, Muffin, and Daisy are heading out in about thirty or so minutes to Shady Tree Park for safekeeping."

Alexis straightened. "Shady Tree? In New South Wales?"

"Can we help?" I asked.

"We'll take all the help we can get," Aunt Mamie said.

Back at the animal clinic, we found three transport crates outside the wombat pen. Alexis gave me a sad smile. "Want to get Boomer first?"

I nodded, and we entered the pen. We searched in each of the burrows, and then I peeked into the hollow log. "Hey, buddy," I said, seeing a wombat bum. "Ready for your helicopter ride?"

At the sound of my voice, Boomer shimmied out of the tight spot and zoomed around the enclosure a few times, sprinting across our feet and showing off.

Alexis laughed. "There goes Bonkers!" She had given him the nickname when he was a small joey in the clinic, where he gained a reputation for racing around recklessly and bulldozing into anything that would make a mess.

Alexis caught him and cuddled him, which was harder

these days, now that the little wombat was not so little anymore. "Oof," she said. "Feels like you've been eating quite a
lot of carrots!"

Aunt Mamie came around the corner with a pile of
towels in her arms. "Thank you, Alexis," she said. "You can
put him in here." She opened the first crate, stuffing a few
towels inside for extra comfort. Alexis lurched over to the
crate as Boomer tried to squirm out of her arms. "It won't
be long before this joey weighs as much as you," Aunt
Mamie said, patting Boomer's belly.

I felt a pang in my chest. "How long until he can come
back, Aunt Mamie?"

She fiddled with the door to his cage. "Hard to tell,
bunny. Days or maybe weeks. Depends on the fire."

I had already learned this summer that the hardest day
for an animal rescuer was the day you had to say goodbye
to an animal you'd grown to love. Aunt Mamie said it was
like giving away a piece of your heart every time. I looked
at all the animals we were sending off today. The wombats.
The birds. The injured echidna in the clinic. All the reptiles
and frogs. Maybe we weren't saying goodbye forever, but
still, my heart ached.

We heard the helicopter before we saw it coming over
the trees. Muffin and Daisy had been coaxed into their own
travel crates, and all three wombats were ready to go. When

the helicopter landed, we were all business. No time for a weepy parting.

"Quite a fire over there," the pilot told us.

"You could see it?" Alexis asked.

"Hard to miss," he said. "It's a monster."

The thought of a monster fire gave me goose bumps and sent a chill up my back as I helped Alexis lift Boomer's crate into the helicopter. It took the pilot, Mrs. Curry, and Mr. Curry all working together to get the bigger wombats into the helicopter. Muffin made a yelling kind of hissing noise, clearly unhappy.

"Easy as you like, Muff," Aunt Mamie said, putting her face to the crate. "Easy as you like." At her voice, Muffin settled down, and we shut the doors.

"All right then, folks," the pilot said, "you keep an eye on that fire, okay? Don't let it get too close before you evacuate yourselves." And then he climbed into the helicopter and flew our sweet wombats to safety.

THE ROUNDUP
Chapter 6

The next morning, Mr. Curry made breakfast for twenty in the bush camp, as volunteers and Bailey Sanctuary neighbors descended on our property to help round up and catch the wild wallabies and kangaroos and emus. The fire was still on the other side of the river, uncontained and swelling by the hour, sending puffs of smoke in our direction when the wind was right. It was time to get the animals out. If the fire jumped the river, there wouldn't be enough time.

Mom stood up from her place at the long picnic table and tapped her coffee mug with a spoon to get everyone's attention. "Excuse me!" she called, using her teacher voice.

The table chatter died down as the volunteers looked up from their plates and focused on Mom.

"As you know, the Wallangarra fire is only about ten miles away, currently being held back by the river," Mom said. "Today we are safe, but our time is running out. Overnight the fire grew by hundreds of acres, and this weekend is calling for higher temperatures, much stronger winds, and dry lightning."

I almost choked on my orange juice. "Dry lightning?"

"Like a thunderstorm without rain," Alexis explained, her face pale. "It can set more fires. And the wind could push the big fire over the river."

"That's why we thank you all for coming," said Auntie Lynette. "We need to evacuate our animals to safety, and we can't do it without your help."

Aunt Mamie was over by the path with Mrs. Curry. "We could use five volunteers up at the clinic," she called. "We've got a few more animals to box up before their transport arrives. There's Mum, our female koala who is not a fan of travel, a litter of delicate pygmy possums, an echidna and a bilby we're still nursing back to health, and a bat who came in last night with an injured wing."

A group of volunteers deposited their cups and plates in the camp sink, thanking Mr. Curry, and followed Aunt Mamie and Mrs. Curry up the hill to the clinic. The rest of us were on the roo-wrangling team.

Alexis and I helped Mr. Curry with the dishes in the sink as Auntie Lynette gave us all a briefing.

"We have a big job," Auntie Lynette said. "This sanctuary is home to hundreds of wild animals. Many of them have learned to trust us as a source of food and safety. So we've called in an expert to help us evacuate them."

A guy wearing a safari-type outfit with a wide-brimmed

hat and hiking boots stepped out of the crowd of volunteers. "G'day folks," he said, tossing back the rest of his coffee. "Rocco here. Any of you folks ever catch a roo before?"

I looked up from the plate I was scraping into the compost bin. Nobody raised a hand.

"No worries," Rocco continued. "First thing we'll do is move all the hay from the feeders around the property up closer to the house. Hopefully you've got some hungry roos, and while they munch on breakfast, we can bag 'em up and move them straight to the truck for transport." He adjusted his hat against the sun. "For the feisty ones, we'll have to get resourceful. Roos and wallabies are quite strong, and if you try to catch 'em, they're going to fight back." Rocco rubbed his head as if he knew this from experience. "I reckon for most roos, we'll need teams of two. One person to grab its tail and flip it upside down while the other bags it up." He clapped his hands together as if this was easy-peasy, no big deal. "If you've got a big bloke, you might need two or three more people to do the job. And if all else fails, hold on to his tail or lie on him until I can get there. Good?"

Alexis handed me a plate to dry. "Lie on them?" I asked.

"That's the official way of catching a roo, it seems," Alexis said with a laugh.

"What about the emus?" asked a volunteer.

"Ah, yes, I'll need a few volunteers for the emu team,"

Rocco said. He reached over to unzip a giant canvas bag and pulled out goggles, thick gloves, arm pads, and the kind of protective cups that boys wear for sports. Alexis and I looked at each other, trying not to giggle.

"You need all of that to catch an emu?" I asked, surprised. The emus around the sanctuary seemed so laid-back, almost friendly.

Rocco raised his eyebrows. "Ever see an emu under stress?"

A volunteer called out, "I once saw an emu kick his leg out and then up and over its own shoulder to bash a bloke behind him. Guy never saw it coming. Bloody forehead and everything."

Mr. Curry clapped Alexis on the shoulder. "How about you and Kira get a head start on organizing the kangaroo pouches and emptying the hay feeders out in the field?"

"Sounds good to me!" I said, happy to avoid getting kicked in the head by a giant bird.

We spent the morning fetching pouches for volunteers and setting up food and water stations for the animals closer to the farmhouse. I dragged a hose from the shed to fill the water troughs, and Alexis used a wheelbarrow to distribute the hay. We even made a little trail of food to lead the animals to the new feeding stations. Rocco and his volunteers caught and bagged up dozens of wallabies and kangaroos. We watched as they carefully hung them in their pouches from sturdy hooks in the back of the truck waiting on the driveway.

By the afternoon we needed more feed, so we headed over to the shed for more roo pellets—and walked straight into a scuffle by the clinic where Rocco and some of the volunteers had a huge kangaroo cornered.

"That's Tank," Alexis told me. He was one of the regulars around the sanctuary, a big red kangaroo. Tank was almost trapped against the clinic wall, but he leaped easily over the nearest fence and into the empty wombat pen, bouncing back out on the other side.

"Someone fetch me the biggest bag you have!" Rocco called, and Alexis and I sprinted into action, grabbing a giant burlap sack from the pile we had collected.

One of the volunteers approached Tank from behind the wombat pen, and the frightened kangaroo bounced away from him and straight toward Rocco, who was waiting quietly near a bush. As soon as Tank got close, Rocco leaped out and grabbed him solidly by the tail, two other volunteers jumping in to help. Once they had Tank on the ground, Rocco lay on top of him to keep him from thrashing. "No stress. No stress," he murmured to the kangaroo, taking the bag from me.

The other two volunteers held open the bag while Rocco lifted Tank up by his tail. Mr. Curry supported the kangaroo's neck, and together they lowered him into the bag.

Aunt Mamie was standing outside the clinic, leaning on her cane, watching.

"Is Tank going to be okay?" I asked her, feeling sorry for the terrified animal.

"We need to be careful with the roos and wallabies," she said. "If they get too stressed, they can overheat, which can damage their brains and muscles."

"Oh, no," I said, certain that Tank must be quite stressed after his ordeal.

"Rocco knows what he's doing," Aunt Mamie assured me. "And their new carers will keep a close eye on them and be able to treat them if necessary."

I turned to Alexis, who had come up beside me. "Let's go check on the animals in the truck," I said to her, and she nodded. We set off toward the driveway, but about halfway there, we stopped. Right in front of the shed, staring back at us almost defiantly, was a scruffy little wallaby.

"Crikey. They missed one," Alexis said, taking a step toward it. The wallaby flinched.

"Do you think we can catch it ourselves?" I whispered, afraid we'd scare the wallaby away if we yelled for help.

Alexis took another step closer. The wallaby startled and turned, about to leap away. And that's when we saw it: she had a joey in her pouch. Alex and I looked at each other. We knew it was up to us to catch her, so that she and her joey could be evacuated.

"It's okay," I murmured in my calmest voice, channeling Rocco. "No stress. No stress."

The wallaby looked ready to bolt at any moment.

"She'll never let us get close enough to grab her tail," I whispered to Alexis.

"The shed has wombat nets," Alexis whispered back. "We could capture her in the net first and then get help."

Out of the corner of my eye, I could see the shed door, slightly ajar. "Good idea," I whispered back. I held my breath as she disappeared into the shed. A moment later she reappeared with a big net at the end of a pole, perfect for catching wombats—and small wallabies, too, I hoped.

I took the net, which was heavier than I expected, wishing I had time to practice netting a wild animal. I had to do it fast, before the wallaby could hop away. *Just one quick swoop*, I told myself, *and the wallaby and her joey will never even know what happened . . .*

The wallaby stared at us, her ears twitching.

"It's okay," I cooed. "No reason to run off into the bush and put yourself in danger. We'll keep you and your baby safe from the fire, I promise." I took a step closer, and then another, the mother wallaby not taking her eyes off me, until I was within netting distance. And then in my mind I counted: *one . . . two . . .*

Before I got to *three*, the mother wallaby took a hop toward the trees and I just went for it, knowing my window of opportunity was closing. I threw the net over the wallaby so fast, I felt a pull in my arm muscles. The wallaby jerked away from me, realizing she was getting caught, and started flailing in the net.

"You're okay! *Shhhh, shhhh*." I tried to soothe her, but she was scared, and it took everything I had to keep her inside my net. Suddenly, in the midst of the tussle, her joey popped up from her pouch, and before I could react, the joey hopped to the ground and slipped easily out of the net.

"No!" I yelled to Alexis. "Grab the joey!"

But the little joey was too fast, hopping away from us into the trees, its mother still stuck in my net—and a bush-fire burning only a few miles away.

TOO QUIET

Chapter 7

As Alexis and I made our beds in the tent the next morning, my heart throbbed at the thought of the empty clinic and all the animals waking up in a new place. Though the fire hadn't yet come, the sanctuary already felt deserted.

"I can't stop thinking about that poor wallaby joey," I told Alexis as I tucked in one of my blankets. What did a baby wallaby do without his mother—hop around the gum trees searching for her? Was it hungry? Scared? Cold?

Alexis sighed. "It's too quiet and sad in this sanctuary. We should have gone with my mum to check on the pygmy possums this morning." The tiny joeys had been settling in nicely with their temporary carers until one of them, the littlest, refused to eat. Mrs. Curry had gotten up extra early to pay him a visit and make sure he was okay.

"You girls mind lobbing in on Evie to bring her some brekky?" Mr. Curry asked, peeking into our tent and holding up a small bag. "She left before sunrise, and I reckon she's hurting for some real food by now."

I hopped up. "Yes! We'll take it." I'd been meaning to visit Evie out in the field yesterday, but after all the evacuation work and then losing the joey, I had felt too exhausted and discouraged.

Alexis and I followed the trail out of the bush camp and through the field, which was empty and still. I even missed the emus skulking around, begging for food and poking their heads everywhere. We stepped over blackened leaves that had been blown here by the wind—a reminder that a huge fire was burning out of control just over the river. We tried to ignore the hazy sky, the blue color dulled by a pale blur of smoke, and the way our eyes watered when the breeze blew the smoke toward us.

We found Evie sitting perfectly still in a cluster of trees, watching the termite mound through her camera with its long telephoto lens. I tried not to startle her as we approached, but when Alex said "Hi!" she jumped a mile.

"Shhh!" she said, a finger to her lips.

"Sorry," I mouthed.

"Did you see the parrot?" Alexis asked in her quietest whisper.

Evie shook her head. "It's not good, mates. Not good at all. Absolutely no sign of any birds."

"They'll come back," I said, wishing Evie wasn't so glum. "They have to come back. They have eggs in their nest!"

Evie sighed. "You'd hope so, right? But that's not always the case. This nest could be abandoned."

"They would leave their babies?" I asked.

"Remember, it's late in the season to find a clutch of eggs," said Evie. "Not entirely out of the question, but the longer I'm not seeing the parents return, the more I'm thinking the eggs aren't viable."

"So if the eggs aren't viable, the parents just leave them there?" I asked.

"It's nature, Kira," Alexis said. "What would you expect the birds to do, have a funeral for their eggs?"

"Don't be ridiculous," I said to Alexis. "Maybe some food will cheer you up, Evie." I held up the bag.

"Too right," Evie said, standing up and stretching. "I've been watching this nest for hours."

We followed Evie back to her tent, and we all sat on the ground on a blanket. The sun was still low, the air not too hot yet. Evie tore into her breakfast. "Please tell your dad thank you," she said to Alex. "This is bonza." She wolfed down her brekky roll, so I figured bonza meant *really good*.

While Evie ate, Alex and I sat there in silence. The bush was too quiet. Even with trees everywhere, we heard no birdsong—no squawking cockatoos or chittering wag-tails—almost as if the bush itself was shutting down. Did the birds know the fire was coming? Had they already evacuated themselves?

"Hey, Evie, is there a chance you might take a break

from research for a bit?" I asked. "I'm not sure you should be out here all by yourself with the fire just over the river."

"The weather is going to get bad over the weekend," Alexis said. "We've already evacuated the animals."

"I can't stop now." Evie finished her sandwich. "Not until I find the birds." Then she got quiet for a moment. "Blimey. Do your aunts think it'll cross the river this weekend, then?"

"They reckon it might," Alexis said.

"I need more time," Evie said.

"Does your cell phone work out here?" I asked.

"Most of the time," she said. "If I remember to charge it."

I groaned. "Evie, what if—"

"If you need to worry about something, mates, worry about all the animals out here. The ones that won't be evacuated. Like sugar gliders and potoroos and antechinus—"

"Ante—what?" I interrupted.

"They're small marsupials. Hard to catch and likely won't be evacuated. I can drive off to safety somewhere and come back when the fire's gone. But the birds and other small animals?" Evie looked grim. "They have nowhere to go."

I thought of the missing joey, a wave of urgency rippling through me.

"But some animals can protect themselves, right?"

Alexis asked. "Echidnas can drop their body temperature, and smaller animals hide in their burrows where it stays cool enough. And some animals even shelter in wombat tunnels. I read about that last year," she added.

"Sure, some animals can survive, Alexis, but what about their habitats?" Evie pointed out. "If my house is gone, I can build another one. If my food is destroyed, I can get more at the grocery store. But what about the wombats? Or the koalas, which only eat one kind of leaf? If their trees are all burned . . ."

I didn't know what to say. Everything felt so full of life in the sanctuary. I couldn't imagine all of it being destroyed by fire.

"And if by some miracle this fire misses us, there will just be another one sooner or later," Evie said. "Climate change causes more drought, which means greater fire risk—which means more animals die or lose their habitat." She paced in front of us, counting each of these terrible things off on her fingers. "Those are just the realities."

The ball of worry in my chest grew. Drought. Fires. Extinctions. I could barely catch my breath. "Evie," I said, "What do we do?"

She stopped in front of us. "If we can find this parrot, then we can apply for a grant to protect it and its habitat— this sanctuary—for the long term, even after Mamie and

Lynette are no longer here. And if the fire comes through this place, they're going to need money to recover from the damage. This parrot—and all the animals that live here—will be relying on us to restore their habitat."

Money for the sanctuary to recover from the fire? Grants to restore the habitat? I hadn't even thought of such things, but suddenly they sounded important.

Maybe we needed this paradise parrot as much as it needed us.

Evie studied the trees around us, which were eerily silent under the smoky sky. "I'm going to take a long bush-walk to see what I can find. And then I'm going to watch that nest. All night if I have to." She gave us a shaky smile. "Don't worry, mates, I know there's a paradise parrot on this property, and I'm going to find it and get us the proof we need."

FINGERS CROSSED
Chapter 8

On our way back to the bush camp, Auntie Lynette called to us from the veranda as we passed the farmhouse. "You two looking for a job?" She came down the stairs and met us on the driveway.

There were piles of equipment spread everywhere: fire blankets and face masks, fire gloves, hoses, shovels, bags of sand, and a stack of giant wheelie trash bins.

"Wow," I exclaimed, awed by the serious-looking equipment.

"How'd we get all this stuff?" asked Alexis.

"The community collected it for us and delivered it this morning," said Auntie Lynette. "Even though we're out in the bush, we have quite a support system of friends and neighbors. Now we need to fill these buckets with sand and load them onto the trailer." She gestured to the sanctuary's small utility vehicle parked nearby. It was attached to a trailer that we normally used for carting around eucalyptus branches or hay bales to refill the feeders.

"Why sand?" I asked.

"To put out spot fires," she explained. "We're going to

station some firefighting equipment around the property. Even if the fire doesn't jump the river, it may spit sparks in our direction when the wind changes, and we want to put out any spot fires quickly. We'll also distribute those new rubbish bins, and Mr. Curry will fill them all with water."

I reached for a tower of buckets. Behind me, Alexis took her own stack. "But if the fire gets too close, we're going to evacuate, right? All of us?" I asked. Seeing all this firefighting equipment made me worry that Auntie Lynette was going to stay behind and try to fight the bushfire herself.

"We'll all be moving to the university at the first sign of danger," Auntie Lynette assured me. "They have a dorm with an empty floor waiting for anyone who needs it. We'll leave firefighting to the professionals." She tossed a few bags of sand onto a pile and ripped open the first bag. "I love this place, but not nearly as much as I love this family."

The thought of evacuating left me with a mixed feeling of relief and hopelessness. How could we leave the farmhouse where my dad's family had lived for generations? Where my grandma and my great-aunt Mamie had grown up? The veranda with the porch swing, where Dad and I used to watch the sunrise? The farmhouse was part of my family, too.

We got to work, and I tried putting aside my worry about fighting fires or evacuating or—I took a shaky breath—finding a baby wallaby that didn't even know it was in danger. I focused on sand and buckets and shoveling.

"Hey, Dad," Alexis called, as Mr. Curry came up the path. He helped us organize the buckets onto the trailer. Auntie Lynette joined us, and the four of us worked for a while together in silence.

"You know something else that stinks about all this?" I announced, taking a break to lean against the trailer, sweat stinging my eyes. "Evie thinks the paradise parrots may never come back to the nest. Even worse, that the eggs might never hatch."

Auntie Lynette stood up. "She still hasn't seen any birds by that nest?"

"Maybe they've left to escape the fire," Alexis said, adding a full bucket of sand to the trailer. "Seems like a lot fewer birds around here today. Maybe they know they need to get away."

"Evie's planning on staying up all night tonight so she can watch and see if they return," I said.

"Evie puts a lot of pressure on herself," Auntie Lynette said, counting the buckets of sand as Mr. Curry shifted things around on the trailer to make more room. "It's one of the reasons she's such a good researcher and one of my best students. But it's not healthy to stay up all night."

Alexis looked at me. "She should use a trail camera."

"What do you mean?" I asked.

"It's a small video camera you can attach to trees," Alexis said. "Dad, remember when you used a trail cam to find out what was raiding the bush camp rubbish bin every night?"

Her father climbed into the driver's seat of the utility vehicle. "That I do. And we discovered it was a quite pudgy possum." With a smile and a wave, Mr. Curry drove off with the buckets of sand, rubbish bins to fill with water, and firefighting equipment to be staged around the property.

Auntie Lynette put down her shovel and motioned us toward the shed. She pulled down a box from a dusty shelf and handed it to me. "Give Evie this trail camera to use." It was only about the size of my hand, a rectangular box with a camera lens right in the middle. "She can mount it near the nest and set it to record any movement. Then tomorrow she can check to see if there was any bird activity by the nest," said Auntie Lynette.

"This is . . . bonza," I said, quoting Evie. "Don't you think, Alex?"

"Too right," Alexis agreed, her eyes sparkling.

Auntie Lynette grinned. "It's also cellular enabled, so as long as there's cell service, which can be a bit wonky out in the bush, Evie can install an app on her phone and check the camera footage anytime, from anywhere."

"Evie will be so glad to have this! Can we go give it to her now?" I asked.

"Go ahead. I'll finish up the rest of the sand buckets for you," Auntie Lynette said, shooing us out of the shed.

"Thank you!" we called over our shoulders as we raced back to the trail and out to Evie's field station.

When we got to Evie's camp, we didn't see her anywhere. We searched by the termite mounds, over at the rock she liked to sit on, and all around her equipment tent, but the camp was empty.

"Evie!" I whisper-called, in case she was silently observing a paradise parrot.

"We have something for you!" Alexis called more loudly, but there was still no answer.

"Could she still be out in the bush?" I asked.

"Maybe we should just set it up ourselves and then tell her about it later," Alexis suggested.

"We can tell her at dinner," I said. "She'll be so happy!"

We installed the trail camera, tightening its strap around a tree trunk near the termite mound Evie had shown us the other day, being careful not to get close enough to disturb the nest. I turned on the camera, pressing the little red button, and we held our breath and crossed our fingers, hoping for cell service. At last we heard a little *bing!* which meant the camera was connected and ready to go.

Alexis looked at the display screen. "One bar," she said, frowning. "That's barely any service at all."

I sighed. "Well, one bar is better than no bars, right?"

When we got back to the bush camp, Alex and I downloaded the trail-cam app onto my phone. Evie didn't return to the bush camp until late, well after we were tucked into our beds. We'd have to wait until morning to tell her about the trail cam. For now, it was up to the camera to do its job. Under my blanket, I crossed my fingers again, wishing for the cell service to stay strong—and for the birds to return to their nest.

EVACUATION
Chapter 9

I woke with a start the next morning, an aching dryness in my throat, after a terrible dream about fires and lost joeys and eggs abandoned in a nest. As soon as I opened my eyes, I realized the true nightmare: the air in the tent was smoky. "Alex!" I croaked. "Alex!"

She jumped out of bed, and we raced for the door and stumbled outside, where the smoke was even worse. I coughed, the smoke coating my throat and the inside of my nose. Everything was dusted in gray ash, and through the trees, the sky glowed an eerie orange-red.

"Mum! Dad!" Alex called. Through the haze we spotted her parents coming out of their tent. All at once, we heard a loud *BEEP, BEEP, BEEP* coming from our phones, making us jump. We knew what that sound meant: The fire had crossed the river.

"Grab your duffel bags, girls," Mrs. Curry cried, running toward us. Mr. Curry was right behind her.

As we hurried to the farmhouse, it was obvious the wind had not only shifted but had grown stronger, blowing dusty earth and smoke into my eyes and whipping my hair into my face. I held my breath until we burst through the front door of the farmhouse.

Everyone was jammed in the kitchen, Mom and Auntie Lynette, Alex and her parents, Aunt Mamie with her cane. Auntie Lynette passed us each a face mask. "I spoke with the fire brigade and the fire is about ten kilometers away at this point—that's around six miles—and it has doubled in size—again. As you can probably guess from the alarms, it's now on our side of the river."

"Crikey," Mr. Curry said under his breath.

"Thank goodness we got the animals out in time," said Aunt Mamie.

"Has anyone seen Evie?" I asked, trying to keep my voice calm.

"No—where is she?" Auntie Lynette asked. "Do not tell me she went out into the bush this morning."

"I never saw her come home last night," said Mrs. Curry. "It must have been very late when she did."

"Her phone might be dead," I said. "Alexis and I can go get her."

"No you won't. I'll go find her, Lynette," Mr. Curry said. "You start wrapping things up over here."

"Okay, everyone check your watches. It's nine fifteen, so let's be out of here by ten," said Auntie Lynette. "The fireys said even with the strong winds, the fire won't likely be here before noon. We need to be long gone by then, so we can drive out safely."

"Girls," Mrs. Curry said, "I need to grab some supplies from the clinic. Please fill the troughs with fresh water for any wild animals seeking hydration while we're gone."

Such as the wallaby joey. I choked in a breath, my heart breaking at the thought of that sweet little creature all alone in a bushfire.

And then the meeting broke apart and everyone went off to do their jobs: Mom and Aunt Mamie gathering up files and maps to bring along, Mr. Curry jogging off down the path to find Evie, and Auntie Lynette hosing down the bushes and grass around the buildings—anything to discourage a flame from taking hold.

Outside, it was dark as dusk, the morning sun nearly hidden behind heavy smoke. It was like being on a different planet, with everything covered in ash, black leaves swirling in the wind. We put on our masks. Would any of this preparation really work to stop this megafire?

"Pull the troughs over here," Auntie Lynette called to us, her voice loud in the still and quiet sanctuary. "You can use this hose to fill them."

Together Alexis and I pushed one of the metal troughs across the dry dirt and out to where Auntie Lynette had set the hose.

I filled the trough with water, staring into the bush, willing the baby wallaby to appear. But the smoke made it impossible to see very far.

I felt Alexis's hand on my back. "You're overflowing the trough, Kira," she said, muffled behind her mask. I took my hand off the nozzle, stopping the flow of water, and swallowed the lump in my throat.

"We still might find it," she said, following my gaze to the bush. She knew I was waiting for the joey. "We still have twenty minutes."

I took a shuddery breath and shook the hair of out my eyes. But I didn't turn away from the bush for a second. Suddenly, I saw something through the smoke. Two people: Mr. Curry and Evie, carrying a giant backpack, her camera and tripod, and a campstool tucked under her arm.

Auntie Lynette glanced up, and then went back to spraying water around the shed. "Good of you to turn up, Evie," she said crisply.

"I'm sorry," Evie said. "I had to check the termite mound one more time." She had dark circles under her eyes, and I wondered if she'd spent most of the night at her field station. "I just need more time," she muttered, to no one in particular.

The way Evie was talking worried me. Would she do something reckless, like run back into the bush until she found the paradise parrot? "You can't stay here, Evie. It's too dangerous," I told her. "We have to evacuate!" She nodded, looking defeated.

Auntie Lynette softened. "We don't have more time, but I reckon you've got plenty of research to report on already, Evie. You'll have a chance to go over all of your field notes back at the university."

Evie frowned. "It's not my research I'm worried about. It's the fact that there's at least one pair of paradise parrots out there, and they're about to face a giant bushfire. And I can't do anything about it."

Nobody had an answer to that.

Aunt Mamie walked by. "Ten-minute warning!"

Auntie Lynette nodded and switched off her hose. "Time to get moving. Kira and Alex, turn off your hose and go get in the van."

My stomach dropped. This was it, the evacuation. We had run out of time.

Evie picked up her heavy backpack and stumbled to the van. Alexis and I went to the shed and turned off the hose. Suddenly, Alexis grabbed my arm. "Kira, look!" She pointed toward the water trough we had just set up.
The wallaby joey was there, drinking.

Relief and fear flooded through me. I looked around for help, but Auntie Lynette had already left. "We have to get him," I whispered to Alexis. "This is our last chance."

"How? We don't even have a wombat net," Alexis said.

The poor little joey was frantically lapping water as if it couldn't get enough, probably dehydrated and hungry from being separated from its mother for so long.

I crept closer to it, the wind blowing smoke into my face and making my eyes sting. With Alexis right behind me, we inched closer and closer until the little joey suddenly stood up from the trough and stared straight at us. We stopped.

"Kira, I don't know about this," Alexis whispered. "We don't even have a pouch."

I motioned for Alexis to stay put and continued on my own, inching closer, hoping the joey might feel less threatened with just one of us approaching. The wallaby miraculously stayed put, and when I got close enough to touch it, the joey let me pet its back.

"It's okay, little one," I said in my calmest voice. I stroked the soft fur, and it was only then, feeling the knobby spine and ribs, that I realized why it wasn't running from me. This joey was more than a little thirsty. It was weak from not eating or drinking since leaving its mother.

"Kira and Alexis!" It was my mom, calling to us from the driveway, where they were loading up the van to leave.

"Let's go, girls!" Mrs. Curry yelled.

EVACUATION

The wallaby startled at the loud voices, crouching as if about to make a run for it. In one fast motion I grabbed him by the tail, right at the base of his rump the way I had seen Rocco do the day we evacuated the larger animals. The joey squirmed, but I took him in my arms, holding him tight against my belly so he couldn't thrash around. He was trembling. "It's okay, buddy," I murmured. "I'm here to help you. Don't worry, we'll get you back to your mama."

I created a little makeshift pouch in my shirt. It wasn't perfect, and if he decided to freak out, he'd likely kick me right in the nose, but somehow he must have known I was a friend to animals, because he settled right down. By the time we were buckled into the van and pulling out of the driveway, the joey was asleep.

A VISIT TO THE SOLARIUM

Chapter 10

The drive to the university was mostly silent as we left the sanctuary to the mercy of the bushfire. Would our farmhouse still be standing when we got back? What about the animal clinic? Would anything survive the fire? My thoughts spiraled into hopelessness as Auntie Lynette pulled onto the highway, leaving our peaceful patch of wilderness behind.

I held the baby wallaby tight in my arms. Beside me, Aunt Mamie checked him all over, inspecting his ears and his little black paws and the mat of fur on his belly. Mrs. Curry had grabbed him a joey pouch and a few days' worth of wallaby formula and pellets at the clinic before we pulled out. Now Aunt Mamie shook up a bottle and handed it to me.

"Just like Blossom," I said when the joey took it greedily.

"Poor little bloke," Aunt Mamie said. "We'll get him reunited with his mum just as soon as we can."

"Have you got a name for him?" Auntie Lynette asked from the front seat.

Alexis, sitting next to me, leaned into me and peered at the little joey.

"Hope?" I offered. "Or maybe Rainy? Because that's what we're really hoping for, right?"

Aunt Mamie scratched the little one between the ears. "I reckon that's the perfect name."

At the university, Alexis and I got our own dorm room across the hall from her parents. Mom's room was next door to ours on one side, and my aunts were on the other. Our room looked out over the quad, a sprawling, park-like area of the campus full of eucalyptus trees, where students strolled and played Frisbee and sat on the lawn with their books.

Staying in a university dorm room should have been exciting, but once we got settled in, putting our few outfits into drawers and laying out our toothbrushes and hair-brushes, we didn't know what to do with ourselves. We sat on our bunk beds, Alexis on the bottom and I on the top, and worried about the sanctuary. Every time I thought about how it might be on fire or already burnt to the ground, I started feeling nauseated. But I just couldn't stop my mind from thinking about it.

Someone knocked, and Aunt Mamie poked her head into our room. "Alexis, your mum took the young wallaby over to the Girraween Animal Reserve to reunite him with his mum. When she returns, we'll all have dinner together at the dining hall."

Alexis and I nodded, relieved that Rainy would be okay.

Auntie Lynette and my mom appeared in the doorway.

"Seems like these two could use a distraction," Aunt Mamie said to them. "I don't think I've ever seen these girls so absolutely silent before."

"I know just the thing," said Auntie Lynette. "Come on, girls—off your beds. Let's go."

I slid off my top bunk, and Alexis and I followed my aunts and my mom out of the dormitory, across the quad, and through one of the old stone buildings to a different courtyard.

"This is the natural history museum," Auntie Lynette said, opening the door for us. "There's one place in particular I think you'll like." She climbed the stairs, past a display of fossils and through a hall filled with specimens of sea creatures, and led us into a big and bright room.

A VISIT TO THE SOLARIUM

"The solarium," she announced. The sunny room was filled with windows and colorful Australian plants, small trees, and big bushy ferns growing green and healthy. All around the room, preserved birds perched on pedestals and branches, just as they would look in nature.

I could picture Evie studying here for hours. Maybe I would study here someday, too.

Aunt Mamie said, "This university has the largest collection of Australian birds in Queensland, right here in this museum."

"Do they have a paradise parrot?" I asked.

"No, but we have a broad collection of parrots," Auntie Lynette said. She went over to a row of tall cabinets lining the far wall of the room and opened one of the drawers.

Alex and I peered inside. The drawer was full of colorful birds lying neatly side by side, each with a tag on its foot.

"Hey, mates," someone said softly. I turned to see Evie standing in the entrance of the solarium.

"Hi, Evie!" I said, trying to sound extra cheerful to make up for the super-serious look on her face.

With a nod, she walked past us and stopped at a tall cabinet labeled "Egg Collection." "I want to compare the eggs we saw to other parrot eggs," she said, scrolling through her phone to find the pictures she'd taken of the eggs in the termite mound.

"Evie," Auntie Lynette said, joining her in front of the drawer of parrot eggs, "you are a dedicated researcher. Don't forget that. You've done your best."

Evie slouched, putting down her phone. "I just needed one good picture of the bird. Just one. That's all I needed to show everyone that the nest belongs to a paradise parrot, so that we could protect it," she said.

Auntie Lynette put a hand on Evie's shoulder. "We cannot stop a bushfire that big from coming through the sanctuary. But birds are surprisingly resourceful. Don't give up hope."

"Termite mounds have been known to fare quite well in bushfires," Aunt Mamie said. "Isn't that right, Lynette?"

"Yes," said Auntie Lynette. "Maybe the eggs will still be there when we return. Maybe the parents will even come back as well."

"But if I had proof right now," Evie said, "I could get you help for the sanctuary—money and grants—to keep it thriving. If the fire comes through, you're going to need money to rebuild."

"Wait," I said, all of a sudden realizing something. "Would a video work?"

Evie frowned. "A video of what?"

I grinned at Alexis. "We forgot to tell her about the trail camera!"

Evie grabbed my arm. "What trail camera? What are you talking about?"

"We installed a trail cam by the termite mound!" Alexis said, jumping up and down.

"You did?" Evie said. "What?" She blinked in disbelief. "When?"

"Last night," I replied. "It was Alexis's idea."

"But when we got there, we couldn't find you," Alexis said, "so we decided to just install it anyway."

"Was it set to record overnight?" Evie asked, her face lighting up.

I nodded. "And if the cell signal was strong enough, we should be able to access the footage on my phone back at the dorm."

Evie slung her backpack on, looking happy for the first time all day. "You girls are geniuses. Let's go!"

At that, Alexis, Evie, and I bolted out of the museum and back to our building on the quad, leaving Mom and my aunts in the dust. Because what if there was a paradise parrot alive and well and captured on video?

I knew it was a long shot. But it was pretty much the only shot we had left.

A PERFECT MATCH

Chapter 11

I dashed up to our room to grab my phone and then met Evie and Alex in the common room on the first floor of our dorm. The room was mostly empty except for a group of students studying together at a table in the corner. Evie paced in front of the big window, but when I sat on the couch with Alexis, she crowded in beside me.

I got the app going, but the connection was slow and when I tapped the files of photos, the entire window froze. I looked at Alex, frustrated.

"Did it work?" Evie chattered nervously, so much relying on whatever we'd find on the trail camera. "Do you think there's a strong enough cell signal out there?"

I swallowed. "It should work," I assured her, but at the same time I felt a twinge of doubt in my chest. What if one bar of cell service wasn't enough? Or what if the fire had already reached the sanctuary and destroyed the trail camera?

I restarted the app, all of us glued to the screen to watch it load up.

Evie kept talking. "I just know they're there, but I can't

prove it. That's the most frustrating thing—"

"Got it," I announced, holding up my phone with a wave of relief. I tapped the link to the recorded footage, and an index with a bunch of time stamps popped up. 5:00 p.m. 5:03 p.m. 5:09 p.m. 5:16 p.m. There must have been twenty-five or thirty of them.

"The trail cam only records when there's movement, which means there was activity around the termite mound at each of these times," Alex said. "So if the parents came back to their nest last night, we'll have it caught on camera."

I clicked on the first time stamp, and we got an up-close-and-personal look directly up Alexis's nose as she mounted the camera. I snorted and let the clip loop for a moment.

Alexis laughed and clicked the next one.

"Just a black fly," Evie said.

The next one showed a bird.

"Kookaburra," Evie sighed.

More flies, falling leaves, a lizard skittering over the camera lens, a purple and red parrot.

"Are paradise parrots nocturnal?" Alexis asked as I clicked on the file time-stamped 11:16 p.m.

Evie shook her head. "Not according to the accounts I've read, but you never know. There *are* two species of noctur-nal parrot—one in New Zealand and one here in southern

Queensland. They're also critically endangered, by the way."

It got quiet after that, both on the trail cam and on our couch as I scrolled past all the late-night time stamps, which most likely belonged to the nocturnal animals.

"That must be dawn," Evie said, pointing to the cluster of time stamps around 6:00 a.m. "Animals are active at sunrise."

I tapped the first one, 6:03 a.m., and gasped. There, standing on the termite mound, silhouetted by the sun rising through the smoke from behind the trees, was a parrot.

"It's a bird," Alexis said. "That's definitely a bird on top of the termite mound."

"It's not just a bird—it's a *parrot*," I informed her. "Look at the shape of the head and body. Clearly, it's a parrot!"

Evie nodded eagerly. "Too bad it's so smoky. Can you zoom in?"

I enlarged the image, but it pixelated, making it impossible to see any details.

"Looks like it has dark wings," I said. "Right? Don't they look black?" The paradise parrot had black wings. But the smoke and low light made it hard to tell the true color.

"Let's not get too excited yet," Evie said, taking a controlled breath. "There are plenty of parrots with black feathers. And who knows if this bird even belongs to this nest. Let's go to the next time stamp."

At the next time stamp, 6:08 a.m., the bird flew off.

"Pause it," Evie said, and I did, zooming in to the parrot in flight.

"It has a blue neck!" I said, my heart beating fast. A paradise parrot had blue feathers on its neck! How many Australian parrots have blue neck feathers? I turned to Evie. "This must be that bird's nest! Because you found that blue feather, remember?"

Evie pulled out her notebook. "Keep it paused for one more second." She scribbled down some notes. "It's possible." She was the picture of calm. "Let's keep going."

I unpaused the video, and the bird flew out of the frame. Evie reached over and tapped the next video. At 6:12 a.m. the bird flew back into view and directly into the little hole in the side of the termite mound.

"Yes!" Evie yelled. "It's his nest!" She high-fived us. "This is good, mates. Oh yes, this is bonza." She was no longer calm. In fact, I'd never seen her so excited.

In the next video, the bird was back on top of the termite mound, keeping watch. This time the bird faced the camera directly.

"Okay, pause it. Zoom in again." Evie leaned into me, staring at my phone.

"Look," Alexis said, pointing at the bird. "The wing. There's no red on the shoulder."

I zoomed in closer, blurring the picture, but I could see that the bird's wing was brown and yellow. Not black and red, as we were hoping.

Alexis slid glumly back on the couch. "Game over. It's not a paradise parrot."

Evie picked up my phone for a closer look, squinting. "Hmm. I'm not sure yet. Can you send these files to me?" She handed my phone back, standing up. "I need to examine these videos more closely. Don't lose hope. This isn't over yet." And then she walked out of the common area.

We didn't see Evie for the rest of the day, and I could barely stand the suspense. Did Evie think it could possibly be a paradise parrot? Was the Bailey Wildlife Sanctuary home to an extinct bird or not?

"I just wish we knew for sure what kind of parrot that was in the video," I said to Alexis after dinner, as we returned to our room.

"Paradise parrots have red shoulders. What more is there to wonder about?" Alexis said, pulling her shoes off and falling back onto her bed.

"Well, the video just wasn't great quality. The light was pretty low, and the smoke was thick. So maybe the color was off. Evie said this isn't over yet. Why else would she say that?" I sat in one of the desk chairs.

"It's not that I don't believe her, Kira. I'm just saying

don't get your hopes up." Alexis brought over her guide to the birds of Australia, plopping it on the desk. She flipped it open to the page we'd bookmarked, with the paradise parrot. "There. See?" She pointed to the illustration. The parrot's feathers were bright red on its belly and at the top of each wing.

I pulled out my phone to compare. I found the video of the bird, pausing the frame where it sat on the termite mound facing the camera.

"Look at the shoulders. In the book, they're red. In the video, they're yellow. That color's definite," Alexis said.

"Nothing is definite yet," I said, getting frustrated. "I mean, what if it's molting? Or maybe it's a female? They're not as colorful."

Alexis looked surprised at the way I was pushing back.

I took a deep breath. "Evie's the expert here. Let's just wait until we hear from her."

"Kira," Alexis said, "I know how much you and Evie want to believe that this is a paradise parrot, but you can clearly see—"

I didn't let her finish. "I'm looking at it from every angle, Alex. That's what a scientist does. I mean, how many birds nest in termite mounds? It's pretty unique to the paradise parrot, isn't it?"

Alex shrugged. "That might be worth looking up."

I did a quick search on my phone for birds that nest in termite mounds in Queensland, Australia. "There's a short list," I told her. "The sacred kingfisher, which is much too small, but it does have blue feathers." I scrolled down further on the screen. "And then—" I stopped.

Alexis took the phone, reading. "Golden-shouldered parrot." She stared at me. "Golden, like yellow, shouldered," she said, dropping my phone back into my hands. She flipped the guidebook to the index, using her finger to find the page she needed.

And I remembered that one day out in the bush with Evie when she had spotted a golden-shouldered parrot while we were bird-watching. Was that the bird that belonged to the nest in the termite mound this whole time?

When we compared the bird from our video with the picture of the bird in the guidebook under the listing for "golden-shouldered parrot," it was a perfect match.

THE PROOF IS IN THE PICTURE
Chapter 12

A commotion outside our window woke me up early the next morning. I blinked awake, sliding off the top bunk, and peeked outside to the quad. A crew of people were putting something together. I rubbed my eyes. Was it a stage?

I heard rustling from Alexis's bunk, but I didn't turn to look at her. Suddenly, I didn't like how she thought she was right all the time, just because she knew more about Australian animals than I did. I didn't like the way she had doubted Evie and accused me of wanting to believe that bird was a paradise parrot. Almost like I would believe something even if it weren't true. How could she think that? I was the observer. I was the one who'd been sitting out in the bush with Evie. Science was about not jumping to conclusions. It was about relying on experts. And Evie was more of an expert than Alexis.

I heard her roll out of bed. "Hey," she said. "You know what we should do?"

I kept facing out the window. "What?"

"How about we go back to the museum together and look at the golden-shouldered parrot? They must have one in the solarium or in one of those drawers. Then we can see for ourselves the true colors of its feathers."

I had to admit, it wasn't a bad idea.

"We should see one in real life," she said. "Before we come to any conclusions, right?"

"Yes," I agreed, glad that Alexis and I were back on the same page. "Let's do it."

We got dressed, ate a quick breakfast in the dining hall with our parents, and then headed to the museum. We wove through students walking to their classes, and I noticed that whole groups of people had their faces painted with little planet Earths or were wearing honeybee headbands. I wondered what was going on, and whether it had anything to do with whatever was happening on the quad.

The solarium was empty when we got there. Alex went to the row of cabinets, while I studied each of the preserved birds on pedestals in the exhibit, searching for a golden-shouldered parrot. I passed a laughing kookaburra, red wattlebird, frogmouth, splendid fairy wren . . .

"Found the parrot drawer!" Alexis called.

I rushed over, pulling up the video on my phone to compare birds.

Alex gasped. "Kira—it's missing."

"Huh? Maybe they just don't have one," I pointed out. "It's endangered, so maybe it's hard to get a specimen—" But when I looked into the drawer, I saw what she meant. There was a spot that was empty except for a tag that said, "*Psephotus chrysopterygius*, Golden-Shouldered Parrot, Katoomba, NSW 2003."

I frowned. "Do you think they took it out for cleaning? Or maybe to fix something, or—"

"Kira." Alex spoke slowly. "Doesn't it seem weird that we figure out the bird in the trail cam video is probably a golden-shouldered parrot—and then a few hours later, the golden-shouldered parrot specimen goes missing from this very museum?"

I rubbed my forehead. "I don't see the connection." What was Alexis trying to say?

"Evie," Alexis said quietly. "*She's* the connection. She wants the bird in the video to be a paradise parrot so badly, she got rid of the golden-shouldered parrot—"

"Are you kidding? Evie wouldn't do that!"

"Think about it," Alexis said. "She doesn't want anyone to figure out it's the golden-shouldered parrot on the video, so she gets rid of the museum specimen so that no one can study it and compare the two birds."

"What? That's ridiculous. Anyone could just search it on the internet!" I said, too loudly in the quiet solarium. "What do you have against Evie, anyway?"

Alexis looked stung, but before she could reply, we heard a noise at the door. We turned and saw Evie herself entering the solarium.

"Hey, mates," she said cheerily. "Up early for a visit to the museum?" She dropped her heavy backpack to the floor. "Everything okay?"

"Oh, we . . . uh," I stammered, not knowing what to say. I stepped away from the parrot cabinet.

"Actually," Alexis said, "we were wondering if you had any updates on the trail cam video?"

"In fact, yes, I do," Evie said, smiling again. "Thanks to your genius idea to set up a trail camera, I was able to capture an image of the parrot from the video and then refine it using imaging software. And guess what?" She grinned. "The bird we saw sitting on top of the termite mound in the video is definitely a paradise parrot—and we now have the picture to prove it!"

"Wait, what?" Alexis said, dumbfounded.

"Really?" I said, hope rushing back into my heart. "How do you know that's what it is?"

"The color, plus the size and dimensions of the bird,"

Evie said. "If you're interested, I can show you."

Size. Dimensions. Very scientific things. Good evidence. I raised my eyebrows at Alexis, but she didn't look convinced.

"How is that possible?" Alexis asked Evie. "The bird on the video doesn't even have the right color feathers for a paradise parrot. It looks like a golden-shouldered parrot."

Evie zipped open her bag and pulled out a binder, flipping to a pocket in the back. "See for yourself."

Alex took the photograph, her eyebrows furrowed.

"Those shoulders look red to me," Evie said. "It took some time to find the best frame to work with from the trail cam footage, but as you can see it's got the coloration of a paradise parrot, not a golden-shouldered parrot." She pulled something else out of her binder: a picture of a parrot specimen from a different museum. A little tag hanging from its foot identified the species as "*Psephotus pulcherrimus*, Paradise Parrot, Brisbane, Queensland, 1902."

Alex handed the photos to me, speechless.

"Wow," I said. "You got this from the trail camera?" The bird on top of the termite mound was so beautiful. I tried to imagine what it would be like to see this colorful bird in the wild. I imagined what it would be like to bring these birds back from extinction.

"Yes, I did," Evie said. "And it's the exact proof we need."

"So, this is it?" I asked her, barely daring to believe it.

"We really did it? We found a paradise parrot?"

"That's right, mate," Evie said with a triumphant grin as I handed her back the pictures. "We did it!"

I looked at Alexis, wanting to share this moment with my best friend, but she was staring at the floor, biting her fingernail and lost in her own thoughts.

Evie tucked the photos back in her bag. "I'll see you girls later," she said. "I've got a few things to do, and then I'm off to find the professor." With a wave and a grin, she left the solarium.

Back outside, Alexis and I blinked in the bright sun, not quite sure what to do next. I felt giddy, ready to bubble over with excitement.

"Want to check out the library?" I asked. "I heard it's a bajillion floors tall, and I'm sure they have a ton of books on parrots . . ." I stopped talking, realizing Alexis wasn't paying attention.

"Are you listening?" I asked. "I mean, this news is huge, right? Evie said she was going to find a paradise parrot, and she did. Did you see that picture? It's unbelievable! And it lives right in our sanctuary! We need to learn every single thing about this bird." I took a breath. "Alexis? Aren't you happy?"

Alex kicked a rock, sending it skidding across the sidewalk. "I'm just . . ."

As she paused, I jumped in. "Super excited? Thrilled?

Stoked? Isn't that what you say in Australia? Stoked?"

"I'm just . . . thinking," she finally said.

"Oh." We passed between two stone buildings and came out at the dining hall where we had eaten breakfast a few hours ago. "What are you thinking about?" And I could tell from her unsmiling face that she was probably not thinking about the same things I was: how I couldn't wait to see Aunt Mamie's reaction when we showed her the picture of the paradise parrot, how the sanctuary would get money to protect the bird and to even fix any damage from the fire, and how we had officially rediscovered an extinct animal. Probably we'd even be famous, at least among ornithologists, like Evie.

Alexis sat down on a wooden bench shaded by a massive tree. "I can't figure it out." She sighed. "Something doesn't seem right. Is it just me?"

I slid onto the bench next to her. "You saw the picture, and it's obviously a paradise parrot. Why don't you want to believe it?"

"I do want to believe it, Kira, but even Evie admitted she touched up the photo."

"She 'refined' the picture," I corrected her. "She zoomed in and made it clearer."

Alexis shook her head. "Kira. She *photoshopped* it. She changed the colors to make it *look* like a paradise parrot."

I flinched at her accusation. "Evie would never do that," I said coldly.

"Of course she would!" Alexis said, pushing herself up off the bench. "Imagine what rediscovering an extinct bird would do for her career! Wake up, Kira."

"Stop it, Alex. You don't know what you're talking about."

She threw up her hands. "It doesn't take a bird expert to know that the bird on the video is not the same bird that was in that picture!"

"You always think you're so right about everything!" I yelled.

"I'm right about this, Kira," Alexis said.

"No, you're not, Alex, and frankly, you're being rude and—a bad friend right now," I added, seething mad.

"Oh, I'm being a bad friend?" Alexis said, keeping her voice low as a group of students walked by. "You've been following Evie around like a lost joey, believing every word she says. Open your eyes, Kira! There's no paradise parrot!"

"No, Alex. You open *your* eyes," I said, my cheeks burning. "You're not the ornithologist here. Evie is!"

Alexis shrugged. "You'll believe anything you want to believe, Kira. Maybe I'm not always the greatest friend—but only the worst kind of scientist ignores the facts."

And then she walked away.

SCIENCE OVER SILENCE
Chapter 13

At first, I followed Alexis, feeling like I had more to say, but eventually I slowed down and gave up. And anyway, why was I chasing her when I wasn't the one ignoring the facts? She was. Evie was the expert here, not her. How could she not see that?

When I got to the quad, I stopped in my tracks. Hundreds of people were packed onto the grass, carrying signs and chanting in front of an empty stage. This must have been the event they'd been setting up for all day. A concert? And for a moment I felt jealous. All these people were here to hang out, have fun, and listen to music. Did they even know that thirty minutes down the road the bush was on fire? Did they even care?

I read a few of the signs:

"The oceans are rising and so are we!"

"Make the planet cool again."

"There is no Planet B."

And then I noticed that the students we had seen earlier,

some dressed up as bees and some with their faces painted, were there with their own signs.

The chanting got louder when someone took to the stage and turned on the microphone. I tried to figure out what they were chanting. It sounded like *something science*. And then a line of people walked past me, and I heard someone clearly yell out, "Science over silence!"

What did that mean?

The crowd hushed as a woman spoke into the microphone. "You are here today because we need to make changes to save the planet!" she announced, and the crowd cheered. "You are here today to fight for your future!" And with that, a big banner unrolled behind her on the stage that said, "Students Against Climate Change."

So this wasn't a concert—it was a rally against climate change.

"The science is clear: climate change is happening now," the speaker went on. "The evidence is all around us. Habitats are disappearing. Our ice caps are melting and sea levels are rising. Pandemics are popping up. Here in Australia, we are having worse droughts, fires, and floods than ever before—but our leaders are not doing enough to stop it. We need to make them listen to the science. We can't afford to be silent." She started chanting, "Science over silence! Science over silence!" Soon the crowd was chanting with her, hundreds of people, one voice.

The sound gave me goose bumps and I wanted to join in, but instead, I choked. Images of our sanctuary swam before my eyes. Evacuating the animals, wearing masks against the smoke, escaping the flames and embers.

"There is a bushfire raging not too far from here, taking thousands of hectares of land every day," the woman continued. Now she had my full attention. She was talking about my fire. "Destroying the habitat that our koalas and flying foxes and wombats rely on for survival." I took a few steps closer to the rally, joining the crowd. "Humans are creating climate change. Burning fossil fuels. Cutting down forests. And humans can make it better. Put your fear aside. Face facts. If our leaders won't listen, we must speak up." It was like she was speaking directly to me.

Face facts.

Put fear aside.

Speak up.

I thought about how Alexis had said I ignored the facts. I thought about Evie's picture of the paradise parrot, and how it was different from the bird on the trail camera footage. How could it be that the bird on the footage had looked so much like a golden-shouldered parrot? And then I wondered, what exactly did Evie mean when she said she "refined" the photo?

Was Alexis right? Was I ignoring the facts?

"If our leaders won't act, it's up to us to show the way!" The woman at the microphone pounded the podium, and the crowd cheered. As she left the stage, the crowd chanted, "Science over silence! Science over silence!" I joined in this time, loud and clear.

I stayed and listened to every single speaker: adults, students, and even a few kids my age. And by the end of the rally, I realized something.

Facts mattered, and I couldn't let Evie show Auntie Lynette the photo evidence if it wasn't real. Not even if it meant the sanctuary would get money to help fix the damage caused by the fire.

Science over silence.

I had to find Evie before she talked to Auntie Lynette. I whirled around, starting toward the building where I knew Auntie Lynette had her office, when I spotted Evie sitting on a stone wall at the far end of the quad. I hurried over to her, pushing through clumps of students and weaving my way through the crowd as the rally broke up.

"Hi . . . I . . . did you . . ." I caught my breath. "Did you talk to Auntie Lynette yet?"

Evie stood up. "I got distracted by the rally. Wasn't it great?! I'm heading over to talk to her now—"

I grabbed her elbow. "Wait."

She paused. "Is something wrong?"

"It's just the rally was talking all about data and facts, and it got me thinking about the trail camera and the photo," I blurted.

She set her bag on the wall. "Want to see it again?"

I shook my head. "What did you mean when you said you refined the picture?" I asked. "Like, you zoomed in? Did you change the focus or the brightness? What did you do?"

"I got us the evidence we need to prove there's a paradise parrot living in the sanctuary." She opened her bag, pulled out a folder, and handed me the photo.

No one could doubt that it was a paradise parrot. The right size and the unique, vivid colors. Perfect evidence. Maybe too perfect. "So this is an honest and real picture of a paradise parrot?"

"Isn't that what it looks like?" Evie took the photo and slipped it into the folder, then put the folder back into her bag, struggling to zip the bag closed. The bag tipped over, tumbling off the stone wall and spilling papers and books out onto the sidewalk. Evie quickly gathered her things and closed the bag, but not before I saw a flash of something green and blue and black and—feathery.

A wave of dizziness hit me.

Evie had a bird in her bag.

She tried to stuff her things back into her bag, but a black wing popped out the side, getting caught in the zipper. Evie was sweating and clearly flustered.

"Kira, listen, it's not what you think," she said, sounding like a total and perfect criminal.

I wobbled, taking a step away from her, nearly bumping into the stream of students leaving the quad. "Is that the golden-shouldered parrot that's missing from the museum?" I whispered, not wanting to believe it. Why would she steal a parrot from a museum? Had Alexis been right this whole time?

"Just let me explain something," Evie said. "I know that you, of all people, will understand." She reached into her bag and carefully pulled out the preserved bird. It had to be the golden-shouldered parrot, but something was wrong. The feathers on its wing that were supposed to be yellow were red—but they looked sort of dull and streaky, without the sheen of the rest of the plumage. As if they had been painted over with a red marker.

My stomach turned. "You *painted* the feathers?"

Evie's face flushed. "Kira. The fire came so fast, I ran out of time. We needed just one good picture of the bird."

I blinked, shaking my head. "So you painted a golden-shouldered parrot to look like a paradise parrot?" I couldn't believe this. "To take a picture?"

"Listen," Evie said quickly. "The woman who spoke at the rally was right. In science, you can't ignore the facts. But it gets murky when you *know* the facts, but don't have the exact right evidence to prove it."

"What?" I said, shocked. "Evie, she said to *face* the facts and speak up for science. Not to *fake*—"

"But we *are* speaking up for science! We *know* there is a paradise parrot on the property. You saw one. Alexis saw it, too. You even heard it on the song meter," Evie said. "We have real data to show. But we were missing the final piece of evidence to really drive home the proof: a photo."

My head was spinning. Suddenly, all I knew for sure was this: Evie, this scientist I had trusted, was lying about her data. It felt like a betrayal in the worst way. I had even defended her to Alexis, my best friend, to the point that we probably weren't even friends anymore.

"Did you or did you not see a paradise parrot on the sanctuary property?" Evie pressed.

"I can't be sure," I told her. I just wanted to leave and go find Aunt Mamie and Auntie Lynette.

"Then think about it this way," she said. "Is there *any chance* that the bird you saw with Alexis back in June, the bird that started this entire search, was a paradise parrot?"

"Yes, of course. We thought it was a paradise parrot—"

"Right. So if there is even a *small chance* that you rediscovered an extinct bird, isn't it our responsibility to protect it at all costs?" She paced the sidewalk. "Just think: Right now, there is a fire raging through the sanctuary—"

I flinched, picturing it. A fire as big as my town back home, eating its way through the bush . . .

"—and the parrot's habitat will be destroyed—but with my data and this picture, we'll get expert help and money to rebuild a home for this bird on your aunts' sanctuary. Don't you see? It's a win-win for everyone—your aunts, the sanctuary, and most of all, the paradise parrot."

My head ached. Of course I wanted to help my aunts, but was this the right way?

"But what if it's *not* a paradise parrot?" I asked.

"What if it *is*?" Evie replied, pacing even faster now. "With no intervention, the last known family of paradise parrots will be—*poof*—gone! Back to extinction." She stopped, pointing a finger at me. "And you could have saved them."

I swallowed.

"I reckon that's not a chance we can take, Kira," she said. "Listen, obviously I'll clean up the stuffed parrot and return it to the museum, don't worry about that." She pulled her binder back out, showing me the picture again. "And when I get back to the sanctuary, I'll take a proper picture when I see the *real* paradise parrot. But, for now, this is what I had to do. Don't you see?"

I took the picture, inspecting it. It really looked like a paradise parrot. Evie had taken a photo of the painted, stuffed golden-shouldered parrot and expertly placed it into one of the frames from the trail cam video. But I felt sick holding this picture of a painted bird, made to look like something it wasn't.

Evie took another step closer to me. "I'm doing this for the sanctuary, Kira," she pleaded. "I'm doing this for the paradise parrot."

I studied the picture again. What if there really was a paradise parrot in the sanctuary? It was still entirely possible. I saw Evie's point: Why not get help now, and then worry about the details later?

Maybe this picture was the answer we needed.

FACING THE FACTS
Chapter 14

I watched Evie leave to go talk to Auntie Lynette. The quad was still emptying, a cleanup crew busily taking down posters, groups of people walking past holding their signs. One kid stopped in front of me. "Science over silence!" He held up a fist and I held up my own in solidarity, but when I tried to say the words, they got caught in my throat.

When I was alone on the sidewalk again, I looked at the banner hanging over the stage and the cardboard signs stuffed into the recycling bin. A wave of regret swallowed me whole.

The picture of the paradise parrot wasn't real.

The bird in the picture was a fake, and that was a fact.

How could I let Evie pass this photo off to Auntie Lynette?

I couldn't ignore this any longer. I had to speak up. I ran, my feet pounding hard against the sidewalk until I reached Auntie Lynette's building. I found her office on the first floor by the fountain, and I skidded through the open door.

Evie was already there.

"Kira!" Auntie Lynette said when she saw me. "What a nice surprise! We were just talking about you."

Evie grinned. "I was telling her all about our findings."

"You—you already told her?" I asked, breathing hard from my run.

"Evie has done some incredible work," Auntie Lynette said, her face glowing. "And she's going to give you and Alex credit for assisting her. After all, the trail camera was all thanks to you girls!"

I felt dizzy.

"Are you okay?" Auntie Lynette asked.

"Evie," I cleared my throat, "can we speak outside for a moment?"

Evie's face dropped. "Now? Really?" She glanced at Auntie Lynette and then back at me.

"Just for a second," I said, trying to lead her out the door.

Evie relented and stood up to follow me. As soon as we stepped into the lobby, she crossed her arms. "What's this about?"

I got straight to the point. "Evie, it's not right to use that picture. It's dishonest and—"

"Slow down," Evie said. "Did you see how excited your aunt was? And she's thrilled that you'll get credit, too. You helped discover an extinct bird at the age of ten!

That's got to be some kind of record."

We stood next to the fountain, the sounds of splashing water and smell of chlorine all around us. I shook my head. "It's still lying. It's not real science."

She sighed. "No, Kira, it's helping a bird. I'm sorry you can't understand that." She leaned toward me, looking at my face. "Do you understand how important this is? For all of us?"

I stepped away from her. "Nothing is more important than the truth, Evie. I have to tell Auntie Lynette."

"Kira, you can't!" She suddenly looked desperate. "You'll get me kicked out of the university! My career will be ruined before I even get started. Come on, Kira—think about the bird! Think about the sanctuary, and all the animals who need our help, and the good that this could do for them!"

I felt my face flush with heat. Why hadn't I listened to Alex when I had the chance? She knew Evie was up to something, and I had refused to listen. Instead, I had trusted Evie. I was so proud to be on her team. So proud to be a part of her research. I thought I wanted to grow up to be a scientist just like her.

I sat down on the edge of the fountain. "Evie, I don't want to do this kind of science."

Evie's face fell, and after a few minutes she walked over

and took a seat next to me. There was a long moment of silence. Then she said, "I don't want to do this kind of science either."

"It's not even real science," I said. "Faking a photograph of an extinct bird is lying."

Evie swallowed. "It's more than lying, Kira. Making up evidence like that is fraud. And it's wrong."

I let a moment pass, watching the water in the fountain spout out of the top of an artistic tower of rocks and into the pool below filled with pennies. If I had a wish right now, it would be that I knew how to get out of this mess.

"I see it now: I let things go too far," she said, quietly. "I don't even know how it happened." She stared at her hands. "It's like I lost sight of what's important. I got caught up in finding the bird. Caught up in being the person to find the bird. I just wanted it to be alive, so I could save it from extinction." She put her hands over her face.

"What are you going to do now?" I asked.

In my mind there was only one thing she could do. Make it right.

"You want me to tell the professor, hmm?" She looked out from behind her hands.

"I think she'll forgive you," I said. Wouldn't she?

Evie sighed. A moment later, she asked, "How about you, will you forgive me?"

I didn't know how to answer that. I wasn't sure which was worse: realizing there was no paradise parrot alive and well on the property—or discovering that the scientist I had admired and wanted to be like when I grew up had committed fraud.

"Yeah, I get it," she said. "Honestly, I'm not sure I'll be able to forgive myself."

We sat for a few minutes longer, and then Evie stood up. "Okay. I guess I have some explaining to do." She took a step toward Auntie Lynette's open door and then peered back at me. "Kira, I hope you know that I am sorry. What I did was wrong and unethical. At age ten, you already know more about what it means to be a scientist than I do."

She gave me a small smile. And then she cleared her throat, took a deep breath, and returned to Auntie Lynette's office.

I didn't stick around. Instead I took a long walk through campus to calm myself down before arriving back at the dorm, where I was afraid Alexis wasn't going to talk to me. I crossed the quad, which was mid-cleanup from the climate change rally, with crews taking down the stage. It looked half broken—just the way everything felt at that moment. Evie. The parrot project. My friendship with Alexis. The sanctuary. Maybe even our whole planet.

When I got to our dorm room, the door was open, and Alex was on her bunk reading a magazine.

"Hey," I said.

She looked up, but only for a moment.

I sat at one of the desks, the chair squealing across the dorm's tile floor. "You were right," I said.

Alex stopped reading. "What?"

"You were right. Evie wasn't being honest." I crossed my arms, suddenly feeling angry. At Alexis for being right. At Evie for falsifying evidence. Most of all, at myself for blindly trusting someone like that.

Alexis tossed her magazine aside and sat cross-legged on her bed. "Wait." She blinked at me. "What?"

"She stole the golden-shouldered parrot from the museum, just like you said. She colored the shoulders red, took a picture, and merged it with a photo from the trail camera footage." I took a breath. "In a nutshell."

Alexis smacked her head with her hand.

"I know," I said.

"I can't believe it," she said, shaking her head. "I just . . . can't believe it."

"You were right, Alex." I took a breath. "I'm sorry I didn't listen to you. I'm sorry that I doubted you. I'm sorry I was such a bad friend."

Alexis still looked shocked from all of this new

information. Speechless, even, which was a rare occurrence for her.

"All of it was just so exciting, you know? Finding a bird that was supposed to be extinct! How amazing is that?" I looked down at my hands. "I loved that feeling."

"You liked it even more than feeding Blossom," Alexis said.

"Maybe sometimes," I admitted. "I do like field research. I know it seemed boring to you, but to me it was like hunting for treasure, plus another way to help animals at the same time."

We were interrupted by a knock on the door, and Mrs. Curry poked her head in. "Teatime in the common room," she said. "Dad has a surprise for everyone."

Alexis bounced out of her bed, and I followed her out into the hallway, not really feeling like tea or any kind of surprises at a time like this. When I got to the common room, I saw Auntie Lynette, filling her teacup with hot water from an electric kettle, and I went over to her.

"Auntie Lynette, what happened?" I asked. "Is Evie okay? Did she get kicked out of the university?"

Auntie Lynette put down her teacup. "Whoa there, my girl." She smiled, pulling me into a hug. "Can I just tell you how proud I am of you?"

I tried to squirm away, knowing I wasn't worthy of this

praise. I had been an accomplice to Evie's fraud until only an hour ago.

"Seriously, Kira. That took a lot of guts to convince Evie to come clean." Auntie Lynette squeezed me tighter. "There's no place in science for fraudulent work. It's something this university takes very seriously."

"You should be thanking Alex," I said. "She tried to tell me something wasn't right, and I didn't want to listen."

"I reckon it's hard for any of us to believe, including me," said Auntie Lynette. "I trusted Evie. She's been my student for several years—one of my best students. It's hard to believe she would do something like this."

Our hug broke up, and we joined everyone else. Auntie Lynette squeezed in beside Aunt Mamie on the sofa. Alex and I helped ourselves to some tea and took two floor cushions around the coffee table, closing off our little family circle.

"Auntie Lynette," I said, turning to her, "what's going to happen to Evie?"

"Well, bunny," she said, blowing on her tea, "that's something I don't know yet. The university has a committee that will decide what to do. In the past, I've seen students put on probation for being dishonest, at which point they have to conduct their research under strict supervision. This can set back a scientist's career for years."

She took a sip of her tea. "Or, she could be expelled." She frowned. "I'm not sure what the university will decide."

Mrs. Curry nodded her head. "Science is a crucial part of understanding our world. Fabricating data is a serious offense."

"I don't doubt she wanted to help vulnerable animals," Aunt Mamie said. "But Evie was so certain there was a paradise parrot on our property that she failed to consider all the possibilities."

"Such as, maybe the paradise parrot really is extinct?" I asked.

"At least until proven otherwise," Aunt Mamie replied with a wink.

Alexis stirred her tea. "I don't mean to change the subject, but my mom said something about a surprise?"

"That's right, possum." Mr. Curry stood up from the couch, grinning. "I have a small surprise for everyone. Now shut your eyes and picture that we're back at the sanctuary, having our afternoon tea on the veranda, kangaroos hopping around and emus checking us out through the railing . . ."

I kept my eyes closed tight, loving this picture, hoping that soon we'd be back there, the uncertainty of it all making my heart throb.

". . . Okay, open!" We opened our eyes. Mr. Curry

was holding up a platter of cake.

Alexis clapped. "Pavlova! Dad—did you—?

"No, it's from the dining hall," Mr. Curry said, laughing. "They just made it fresh and let me have some as takeaway."

"Well, it won't be as good as yours, but I guess I can make do." Alexis made grabby hands at the platter, and we all laughed.

Mr. Curry passed us each a slice on cafeteria plates, gooey goodness heaped with whipped cream and strawberries with a crunchy meringue crust. And after all that had happened and all that had changed, this one small reminder of life back at the sanctuary somehow helped me feel whole again.

DREAMS FOR THE FUTURE

Chapter 15

A few days later, Aunt Mamie and Auntie Lynette were told that the fire had passed and it was safe to visit the sanctuary. We loaded up into the van and took the long ride back, my stomach flipping and flopping the entire way. Had the sanctuary survived the fire? Was the animal clinic still there? Would Alexis and I be able to return to our Wallaroo tent?

The adults listened to fire updates on the radio, while Alexis and I looked out opposite windows. I watched the landscape as we passed a big field, hoping to see some kangaroos, but it was empty and quiet. We drove through an area hit hard by the big fires of 2020, the trees black and brittle, but I noticed that the ground was a sea of healthy green grass, and many of the damaged trees had sprouts growing out of their bark and branches. Even after such a big fire, the bush was regrowing. Seeing this planted a seed of hope in my heart.

We drove for a while and eventually passed a Bailey

Wildlife Sanctuary sign on the road. As we turned onto the farmhouse's gravel driveway, I held my breath. I wasn't ready to see what had happened to this place. What if it was like Auntie Lynette's beach house in Rosedale? What if everything was gone? A bubble of fear rose into my throat, and I reached for Alexis's hand.

Auntie Lynette parked and turned off the car, but nobody moved. It seemed we were all feeling the same way. Finally Aunt Mamie flung her door open. "Let's get this over with."

We poured out of the van, and I held tight to Alexis so we could stay together. The burned smell was overpowering. I kept my head down, staring at my shoes on the gravel driveway, afraid to look. But I could hear everyone's reactions. Their sharp inhales. A moan. A gasp. A sniffle. I knew it was bad.

I peeked through one eye and saw the field and beyond it the bush, blackened and bare. The gum tree forest that had been lush and green only days ago was a skeleton of trees. I sucked in a breath and turned around to face the farmhouse.

"Crikey," Alexis whispered.

Half of the farmhouse was missing. One whole side of the house had collapsed, leaving the farmhouse that had been in our family for more than a hundred years in shambles. It was worse than I had imagined. I pulled my mom and Alexis closer, stepping over charred debris, my shoes covered in ash. I had to see the veranda.

"It's gone," I moaned. "The veranda is gone." So was the porch swing, where Dad and I had watched so many sunrises.

"How can we have teatime on the veranda without a veranda?" Alexis said plaintively. "Where will we eat our pavlova now?"

I hugged her, remembering all the times we had sat there together, watching the emus and kangaroos.

With all the leaves singed from the trees, I could see straight through to the bush camp. The grill was half melted, the little wooden porches in front of each tent reduced to piles of burned wood, the tents gone completely. The flowy purple curtains Alexis and I had added to her Wallaroo tent on my first night here were now just a memory. Only the concrete shower house was still standing, though it no longer had a roof.

"Look," Alexis said, pointing toward the clinic. She dropped my hand and sprinted down the path.

"Be careful, Alex!" Aunt Mamie called after her.

We could see from where we stood that the clinic hadn't fared much better than anything else on the property. The pens were gone. The metal building had collapsed. Part of the roof sliced the ground at an unnatural angle. The rubble still smoked.

Alexis stepped onto the debris.

"Stay back, Alexis!" Mrs. Curry called after her. "You could get hurt!"

But Alexis wasn't listening. Teetering on a concrete block, she reached down and picked something out of the rubble and held it up. It was a piece of wood with the words *Joey Nursery*—the sign that had hung over our favorite spot in the clinic. It was charred and cracked. Alexis hugged it tight to her chest as if it was the only thing that mattered.

I felt overwhelmed by the devastation. Mom and I were visitors here and could head back to our apartment in Michigan, where everything was still in its place, undamaged and unscorched. But for my aunts and the Curry family, this was their home. What would they do? Auntie Lynette had already lost her beach house from when she was a kid. And now she had lost her beloved sanctuary, too. And Aunt Mamie had lost the house she'd lived in her entire life.

As we turned back to the driveway, I stayed with Aunt Mamie, who walked slowly, leaning on her cane. The fire had damaged so much of the property, more than I had expected, and one question sat so heavy on my chest that it was hard to breathe. Was this the end of the Bailey Wildlife Sanctuary?

"Aunt Mamie?" I asked.

She stopped and looked at me. "Yes, bunny?"

"What are we going to do?" I swallowed against the acrid smell of smoke wafting from the destroyed buildings.

Aunt Mamie kissed me on the forehead. "I reckon there's only one thing we can do."

I held my breath for what she'd say next.

"We're going to get this mess cleaned up so that we can rebuild," Aunt Mamie finished, and my heart started beating again. "We've got to, for the animals."

I thought about the forest of blackened trees on our drive here and how just after a year, there was grass for the kangaroos to nibble, and the gum trees were already growing new leaves for the koalas to eat. A habitat destroyed by fire didn't mean it was lost forever.

"It's not going to be easy," Aunt Mamie continued. "It's going to take a while, and it will be hard not to linger on all that was lost." She put her arm over my shoulder. "But we Baileys are tough, my dear, and we care deeply about this land. We want it to be here for the next generation." She gave me a meaningful look, and I realized she was talking about me.

Her words made me think about the climate change

rally. Those students had made me believe in a vision of everyone coming together to help save something they cared deeply about. If it wasn't too late to save the planet from climate change, then it wasn't too late to save our sanctuary.

"I wish I could stay here and help," I said, knowing our visit to Australia would soon be over. Mom would return to teaching, and I would start middle school.

"Come next summer, I'm sure there'll be plenty of jobs here for you to help with, bunny," Aunt Mamie said, giving my hand a squeeze.

Alex appeared on the trail in front of us. "Oh, hey, I was looking for you." She held up the sign that she had salvaged from the clinic, pulling it apart into two uneven pieces, and handed me the piece with the word *Joey*.

"You're giving this to me?" I asked.

She nodded. "It was already kind of breaking apart. This way I figured we could share it."

I turned it over in my hand, picturing the sign hanging over the joey nursery in the clinic, and blinked back tears.

She held up the other piece, and we joined our pieces together. They didn't meet perfectly, the ends a little too jagged from the damage, but you could still read the sign.

I knew exactly where I would hang my piece up in my room back home in Michigan. Over my favorite window,

where I'd be reminded of my best friend, Alexis, every single day.

Aunt Mamie, Alexis, and I walked slowly toward the others, who were waiting for us by the van.

"I wonder how our termite mound did in the fire," I said.

"I wonder how Evie is doing," Alexis said as she stepped over a fallen branch, blackened from fire. "She messed up, but I know her heart was in the right place."

I paused. Evie's passion for saving animals was a good thing, but that didn't make her bad decisions okay. I turned to Alex with a sudden idea. "Maybe when I come back next summer, we can do our own search for the paradise parrot. But the real and true way, using good science only. And keeping our minds open to all the possibilities."

"I love that idea!" Alexis said, her face lighting with joy.

Aunt Mamie nodded. "Good on you, girls. Just because the hypothesis wasn't proven doesn't mean we have to stop the search."

We found everyone sitting on the little hill by the driveway, quietly looking out over the sanctuary, and we joined them. Nobody seemed ready to leave yet.

Aunt Mamie carefully perched on a flat rock beside Auntie Lynette. "We'll need a bigger clinic this time around," Aunt Mamie said, pointing her cane to where the animal clinic lay in pieces. "More room in the nursery, so we can take in more orphaned animals. And maybe a separate room for squawky parrots."

"What about a pool in the bush camp for the really hot days?" Alexis asked with a hopeful smile.

"Crikey, it won't take me three minutes to fill up a water trough for you," Auntie Lynette said. "There's your pool!" And everyone laughed.

"First things first: I'll start by building a new picnic table for the bush camp," Mr. Curry said. "Just thinking about all this work is making me hungry."

"With a nice big awning for shade at lunchtime," Mrs. Curry put in.

"Why not," Aunt Mamie said, standing up. "Anything is possible, my dears."

The sky was turning the orange and pink colors of dusk. "Sunsets are extra colorful after a fire, thanks to the tiny smoke particles still in the air," said Aunt Mamie. "We can always look for the beauty in any moment, even the hardest ones."

We admired the sunset, and then headed to the van, each of us with big dreams for the future.

Rebuilding the sanctuary would be hard and would take a lot of time and money and muscle power, but I knew one thing: No matter how big the task, when people came together, they could do anything. Evacuate a sanctuary full of animals. Rebuild a bush camp and a veterinary clinic. Stop climate change.

So maybe I wasn't sure exactly what kind of scientist I wanted to become. A veterinarian? A research scientist studying animals in the wild? Or maybe even a climate scientist?

Whatever I did, I was going to be the kind of scientist who told the truth, no matter what.

GLOBAL
Changemakers

Girls like you are speaking out and taking action against climate change.

As Earth's climate gets warmer, girls across the world get louder. News about rising sea levels, extreme weather, droughts, floods, and wildfires has left young people thinking, *Why aren't grown-ups doing anything?* Kids are fed up, and they're making their voices impossible to ignore.

One voice—from a girl named Greta in Sweden—resounded around the world in 2018 when she skipped school to protest. Soon, kids all over the world were striking from school on Fridays, walking out of their classrooms or holding signs outside government buildings to demand action to stop climate change. It became known as the Fridays for Future movement, and it leaped across the world like a powerful fire—but a fire for good.

The next year, young people organized a wave of climate change protests all over the world. The biggest one took place in September 2019, when four million people—mostly kids and teens—marched in 150 countries for a healthier planet. It was the largest climate strike in world history. Kids sent their message loud and clear: We demand action *now*.

The voices of young people are stronger than ever, and adults are listening. Whether you're protesting for climate justice, writing a letter to a leader, helping install solar panels at your home or school, or giving a climate change presentation to your class, your message is changing the world. Even the smallest actions can make a big difference.

Check out these stories from real girls using their skills and passions to help make a difference for the Earth.

A WILDFIRE GOT
Alexandria V.
FIRED UP FOR CHANGE

When Alexandria was thirteen, she was visiting family in California when a terrible wildfire broke out. Even though she was almost 100 miles away, the smoke was thick enough to give her an asthma attack. "My chest started to get prickly, as it does with asthma," she said. "I felt like needles were pinching my chest." She had to return home to New York City early to escape the smoke.

After some research, Alexandria learned that climate change causes wildfires to become more intense and frequent, and that climate change is causing higher rates of asthma in kids. Inspired by Greta in Sweden, Alexandria started protesting outside the United Nations building in New York City every Friday. She started out alone, but before long her activism bloomed into something bigger than she ever imagined. Soon she was working with activists all over the world and helped organize the 2019 global climate strikes. She even gave a speech at the United Nations—the same building she protests outside of every Friday!

Alexandria and Greta are friends now, and they've joined fourteen other kids to file a lawsuit against five high-polluting countries. They refuse to stop their activism until governments take the urgent actions necessary to save the world from climate change.

Reshma K.
INVENTED A TOOL TO HELP PREDICT FOREST FIRES

Reshma lives in San Jose, California, where climate change is making wildfires more common. The fourteen-year-old did some research and learned that the tools scientists currently use to predict fires are slow and expensive. If fires could be predicted sooner, she realized, firefighters could control them more easily and people would have time to evacuate.

Reshma thought of an idea to use information such as humidity, wind speed, soil moisture, and temperature to predict when a fire was likely to break out. She created a computer model, tested it, and kept improving it.

For a science contest, Reshma made a video to educate people about wildfires and explain how her model could help. She ended up winning the Improving Lives Award. Says Reshma, "My parents have always taught me that I may be a kid, but my dreams never need to be small!"

Bria N.

USES HER ART TO HELP ENDANGERED ANIMALS

Bria, fourteen, loves to paint and draw, and she also loves wild animals. So she started an organization, Faces of the Endangered, to protect endangered species through the sale of her artwork. So far, she has created more than 300 paintings of animals, including wolves, whales, tigers, cheetahs, and manatees. "I paint faces of animals that could disappear forever," Bria says. "I feel if people see animals the way I do, we could all save them together." She donates the money she earns to organizations that help endangered species.

Before launching an art project, Bria studies at the library to learn about the animal she wants to paint. When she finishes a painting, she writes a description of the animal and takes a photo of her painting. Then, with help from her mom, she posts her artwork for sale online. She's raised and donated over $70,000 since she started. "We can all do little things to make our planet a better place for people and animals," says Bria.

Genesis B.
FIGHTS CLIMATE CHANGE WITH DIET CHANGE

Like Bria, Genesis also loves animals. Now thirteen, she went vegan when she was six because she couldn't bear the thought of hurting animals. (A vegan is someone who doesn't eat meat or any product that comes from an animal, like milk or eggs.) After some research, she learned that a veggie-based diet could protect the planet, too. So Genesis got her whole family to stop eating animal products. Then she started giving speeches about fighting climate change with a vegan diet.

"It takes up to 1,300 gallons of water just to produce one hamburger," she said in a TEDX speech when she was ten. "That's equivalent to almost two months of showers!"

Now Genesis talks to friends, teachers, and leaders about how eating animals impacts the environment. She even challenged Pope Francis to go vegan! (He didn't, but her request convinced a lot of people to eat less meat.)

"I have to make a difference today and I have to make a difference tomorrow," Genesis says. "Because if I don't, we're just running out of time."

MEET AUTHOR
Erin Teagan

Erin Teagan has a background in science and uses many of her experiences from the lab in her books. To write Kira's story, Erin went to Australia, where she worked as a ranger for a day at a wildlife park. While she was there, news in Australia buzzed with talk of climate change. People worried about bushfires and the threat to plants and animals. Unfortunately, a few weeks later, bushfires began burning millions of acres. Several of the places Erin visited were destroyed by bushfires in November and December 2019.

Another part of *Kira's Animal Rescue* was also inspired by real events. In 2013, a naturalist named John Young announced he had rediscovered an extinct bird called the night parrot in a remote area of Queensland. The photos and video he took provided the first evidence of a living night parrot in nearly 100 years. It was the discovery of a lifetime! He recorded a bird call and found a feather and a nest of eggs. But scientists started to see inconsistencies in his evidence. For example, the eggs he photographed looked clay-like and were in a nest that wasn't the right kind for a night parrot. Could John Young have faked his evidence? He says he didn't, but experts at the Australian Wildlife Conservancy decided his work was fraudulent.

Erin is author of American Girl's *Luciana* series. She also wrote *Survivor Girl* and *The Friendship Experiment*. She lives in Virginia with her family, a hound dog named Beaker, and a bunny that thinks he's a cat. Learn more at www.erinteagan.com.